"Xavier? Is that you? You're... you're alive."

The shock in her voice was clear even though her voice was low.

Xavier's thoughts whirled. Her voice and the large eyes belonged somewhere in his brain, but he couldn't link her up to any useful memories. Stuck between confusion and euphoria, he wasn't sure what to do. "You're not my sister."

She gasped. "No."

He could hear the hurt in that simple word. This was someone he should know, but he couldn't even see her.

"Xavier." In slow motion her petite form started crumpling.

He rushed forward to catch her before she hit the edge of the porch.

A heavy beat of blood pounded against his skull, and his vision blurred to the point he had to close his eyes and hold the sickness at bay. But there was a rightness he hadn't experienced since he'd woken up from the ambush.

Who is she? Should he leave?

No. For that moment she was in his arms, it was right.

He was finally where he belonged...

A seventh-generation Texan, **Jolene Navarro** fills her life with family, faith and life's beautiful messiness. She knows that as much as the world changes, people stay the same: vow-keepers and heartbreakers. Jolene married a vow-keeper who shows her holding hands never gets old. When not writing, Jolene teaches art to inner-city teens and hangs out with her own four almost-grown kids. Find Jolene on Facebook or her blog, jolenenavarrowriter.com.

Books by Jolene Navarro

Love Inspired

Cowboys of Diamondback Ranch

The Texan's Secret Daughter
The Texan's Surprise Return

Lone Star Legacy

Texas Daddy
The Texan's Twins
Lone Star Christmas

Lone Star Holiday
Lone Star Hero
A Texas Christmas Wish
The Soldier's Surprise Family
The Texan's Secret Daughter

Love Inspired Historical

Lone Star Bride

The Texan's Surprise Return

Jolene Navarro

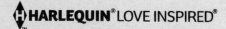

Recycling programs
for this product may
not exist in your area.

LOVE INSPIRED BOOKS

ISBN-13: 978-1-335-47952-5

The Texan's Surprise Return

www.Harlequin.com

Printed in U.S.A.

Now the God of hope fill you with all joy and peace in believing, that ye may abound in hope, through the power of the Holy Ghost.
—*Romans* 15:13

Dedicated to Granner (Jo Ann Hutchinson).
You are an inspiration as you go strongly
into your nineties. Most important,
you have shown me to trust God even when the
storms of this world threaten to pull you under.
Love you, Granner.

Chapter One

Selena De La Rosa sighed and leaned against the old barn wall as she slipped off her heels. Except for the torturous shoes, the day had been perfect for an outdoor wedding and the family Christmas photos. The love she saw in Elijah's eyes when he recommitted his life to Jazmine melted her heart in a way she didn't think was possible anymore.

The weathered wood and the hundreds of tiny white lights, along with the mild Texas temperatures, created the ideal setting for both. Her twenty-two-month-old triplet boys now romped around with the stars of the show. Five baby goats in Christmas sweaters. Who could resist such cuteness?

An idea hit, and she pulled out her phone to make some work notes under her file labeled "Christmas by the Sea." The big plans and budget items for the city were already set in motion, but she was constantly thinking of ideas and adding to her to-do list.

This project was two years in the making and, when it was all said and done, not only her boys but the whole town of Port Del Mar were going to have the Christmas she had dreamed of as a child. This was just the beginning; each year it would get bigger.

There was a tug on her formal dress. "Carry you." Oliver, the smallest of her triplets reached his hands up to her.

Smiling down at him, she put the phone away and brushed a few strands of hay out of his hair. She couldn't bring herself to correct his pronouns. They wouldn't be babies forever.

They would never feel second place to her work either. Ever.

Lifting him up, she rubbed her nose against his sweet baby neck. A small goat in a red-and-green sweater jumped sideways at him, little bells softly jingling. Oliver giggled and snuggled closer to her.

Sawyer, the most energetic of her boys, laughed and ran with three other baby goats. His energy was still unbelievably high after the long day.

Finn, the oldest triplet, was almost down for the count. Cuddled between two identical white-and-brown goats, he whispered something very important as he fought to keep his eyelids open.

Selena took a picture of him with her phone.

"That is just cute kid overload." Her sister-in-law Belle walked in, her elegant dark red gown looking out of place in the barn.

"The goat kids or the human kids?"

Laughing, Belle closed the sliding barn doors. "Both. I think the pictures we took earlier will be my favorite photos ever. We took our family Christmas pictures to a whole new level." She picked up Sawyer and tickled him. "I can't believe this one isn't tired. They stole the show today during the wedding. If you'd let me share that video of them walking down the aisle with their happily-ever-after signs, it would go viral."

"No social media. You know what Xavier would say about that and why." She still had a hard time believing her husband had been gone for almost three years. This would be her third Christmas without him, but she had the boys and his family.

She kissed Oliver on the head and he snuggled closer. "My dad will be here in a moment to get the boys. Since our niece is staying with us, he's taking your girls, too. They can have a big cousin sleepover." She placed her hand on Oliver's back and felt his heartbeat. Growing up she had always been alone. Now, because of Xavier, she had this big family that would always be here for her and the boys.

Belle shook her head in disbelief. "That's six kids. Can Riff handle that many at once? I have no problem keeping Rosie while Elijah and Jazmine are on their honeymoon."

"The girls help out a lot with the boys. Plus, years of managing high-maintenance musicians on the road prepared my dad for handling kids. Who knew?"

"God did." Belle grinned as she sat on the ground next to Finn, Sawyer in her lap. "He prepares for us when we don't even know we're going to need it."

Selena smiled. "I always dreamed of a house full of kids. Before we got married I used to tease Xavier that I wanted enough for a basketball team."

Belle's smile dimmed as she hugged the two boys closer. Selena hated seeing the light turn to sadness at the mention of her brother. "Don't be sad. He was doing what he loved, and he did give me three of the cutest boys ever. It's Christmas. Only joyous thoughts. He'd want you to be happy."

"He'd want you to be happy, too." Both women watched as Finn kissed a sleepy goat on its nose. He was singing a lullaby. Belle smiled and stood. "So, no more gloom. All good cheer from here on out. This will be the best Christmas ever. Starting with the best Christmas cards ever."

Running from her, Sawyer tripped over his own boot and flopped headfirst into the hay. He glanced at Selena, waiting to see her reaction. With a big smile she reassured him it was fine. Giggling, he got up and went after the goats again.

Chasing him, Belle laughed as she swept him up and tickled him. "Your daddy would be so proud of you and your brothers."

"Daddy!" Sawyer clapped.

Selena's heart melted a little at the thought they would never meet him, but they would be surrounded by the people who had loved him and whom he had loved.

As if reading her thoughts, Belle kissed Sawyer's cheek. "We'll make sure your little guys know what a hero their daddy was."

"Dada, Dada!" Now all three boys chimed in.

Her father joined them and together they got the boys' paraphernalia into the Suburban. Her nieces chatted nonstop as all six kids were buckled in. Oliver was asleep before they had finished.

"Are you sure about this? I can go with you," she offered again. "There are several people that stayed to help clean."

"No, no. We're good," her father said. "The girls will help with the boys. Besides, you know they'll be out before we leave the ranch road. You stay and hang out with the grown-ups. Have some fun. You act like an old lady.

Buelita has more of a social life than you do, and she's ninety-three."

"I have a social life. I'm very busy."

"No, you work a lot. It's not the same. Jesse asked me about you again."

She sighed. "He's a pastor. That's his job."

"He's the youth pastor, and he likes you. He stayed to help clean up tonight. Be nice. Say hi."

Knowing she wouldn't win this argument, she kissed him. "Love you. I'll be home soon."

He shook his head as if she was a lost cause. "Not too soon."

She rolled her eyes, then moved to the steps and watched as the taillights disappeared down the long ranch road.

Everyone seemed to be ready for her to move on. Smiling, she crossed her arms against the cold and stood amid the blinking lights. Christmas lights always made everything better.

The velvet night sky was full of God's points of light. Darkness could not coexist with light, so she had to keep the light burning bright for her family. The De La Rosas had had their fair share of darkness growing up. This Christmas was for them also, the happily-ever-after they all deserved.

As she was halfway up the steps, headlights swept across the porch, and Selena stopped and turned. Who could be coming so late? For a second, her heart kicked up a beat. What if something had happened to her father and the kids?

No, there hadn't been enough time for them to even get off the ranch. It had to be a wedding guest who forgot something.

* * *

The sheriff put his SUV in Park behind a row of vehicles parked along the driveway. "I forgot about the wedding." His deep Texas drawl was slow, as if he was speaking to a scared child. "Elijah and Jazmine remarried. It should be over by now and it looks like just a few cars are still here. Sorry, Xavier. I can take you back to town."

Xavier. Xavier De La Rosa. The name still sounded foreign. After more than two years of being a hostage called Pedro Sandoval he was having a tough time adjusting. They said it had been a mistaken identity, but recalibrating wasn't coming easy. He blinked. Everything was out of focus.

He'd be insulted by the sheriff's tone if he didn't feel like a lost six-year-old who didn't know his mom's real name. Then it hit him. *Cicia.* That had been his mother's name, but she was gone. She had died before he was in high school. A wave of fresh grief hit him.

The long porch invited him to come closer. This was his family ranch, and yet there was a scared kid inside him afraid to go into the unknown. There were secrets waiting. The only person he remembered at all was his sister, Belle.

No, that wasn't right. The sheriff said the woman was his cousin. He closed his eyes. Why did he think of her as his sister?

Three deep breaths refocused the blurred images darting in his brain. The scared little boy inside him wanted to run. But that house held the answers he needed to piece his life together.

"Xavier?" Sheriff Cantu's voice broke into his thoughts.

"No." His hand went to the door handle. "We're here. It's better that I meet everyone at once."

Without waiting for the man next to him, he stepped out of the car. He would face his problems head-on. The quicker he gathered the information he needed, the faster he could return to Colombia. Why? He didn't know. That's what he hoped to learn here. He wanted answers and sitting here was not going to get him anywhere.

White Christmas lights wrapped every tree trunk and hung from the branches. More lights trailed along the fence going to the house. Wreaths with giant red bows hung on the posts. Even the surrounding barn was straight out of a winter wonderland storybook.

The roof to the single-story ranch house was outlined with blinking blue, green and red lights. White bulbs hanging like icicles dripped from the eaves.

The pressure throbbed against his skull. Frowning, he tugged his gaze away from the decorations. He hadn't had a headache in two weeks.

It wasn't even Thanksgiving for a few more days, but the place screamed Christmas already. So, this family of his loved the holidays. That would be about right for the way his life was going.

A new piece of information popped up. He discovered something about the man he used to be. Xavier De La Rosa wanted nothing to do with the Christmas season.

A woman in a long gown stood on the steps of the deep porch. His throat went dry as muscles tightened around his airway. "Belle?" He managed one word before the ability to talk left him again. Something wasn't right.

The sheriff caught up with him at the bottom of the steps. "Wait up, Xavier." The man placed a hand on his shoulder.

He stopped, but he kept his gaze on the woman silhouetted by the porch light. She was a tiny bit of curvy femininity. Not Belle.

Her hand went to the heavy post as she moved forward. For a moment the lights showcased her face, highlighting the curves and flawless skin, but then his sight went sideways. Narrowing his eyes, he refocused, but it didn't help.

"Xavier? Is that you? You're…" The shock in her voice was clear even though she spoke low. "You're alive."

His thoughts whirled. Her voice and the large eyes belonged somewhere in his brain, but he couldn't link her up to any useful memories. Stuck between confusion and euphoria, he wasn't sure what to do. There was one thing he did know. "You're not my sister."

She gasped. "No."

Great. He could hear the hurt in that simple word. This was someone he should know, but he couldn't make out the details of her face.

"Xavier." In slow motion her petite form started crumpling.

He rushed forward to catch her before she hit the edge of the porch. One hand held her arm as the other went to support her back. He eased her down and sat next to her, the strange woman leaning against him.

A heavy beat pounded against his skull and his vision blurred to the point he had to close his eyes and hold the sickness at bay. But she was so warm and fit perfectly in his arms. There was a rightness he hadn't experienced since the morning he woke up for the ambush.

Who is she?

Her free hand pressed against his chest, over his heart.

The touch was affectionate and solid, even though she trembled. Should he leave?

No. For that moment she was in his arms, it was right. He was finally where he belonged. He knew that voice.

Under his palm, her ribs were expanding and retracting in short, hard pants. She didn't lose consciousness, but he worried she was going into shock.

The sheriff crouched in front of them, his hands taking the small hands of the woman that belonged to Xavier. He shook his head. Where had that come from?

"Breathe, Selena." Cantu's voice was low and steady. "I'm so sorry about this. He arrived at the station and wanted to come out to the ranch. I thought it would be easier to get everything straightened out with Belle first, then have her tell you. He has memory loss and doesn't—"

"It *is* you." Wonder coated each of her words. Warm fingers touched his face. At first, he pulled back, but then he allowed her to explore him. Her slender fingers pushed his hair back, then went to his shoulder. Tears slipped from her eyes, her touch slowly trailed down his arm, as if making sure he was real.

He held still. She knew him. The soft sounds of surprise mixed with short bursts of nervous laughter.

Sheriff Cantu cleared his throat.

"Xavier, this is Selena." Cantu stayed in front of her, his hand on her knee, but his gaze stayed trained on Xavier. "She's your wife."

His gaze darted to the sheriff, then back to her even though he couldn't make out any details. "Wife?" Had he been able to get the word out?

She shook her head, as if trying to clear it. "I don't

understand. The security company you worked for told us you were dead."

"I.D. had been switched between Xavier and a Colombian named Sandoval. The rebel thought he was Sandoval and he didn't know who he was." Cantu placed his hand on her shoulder. "Is Elijah still here? Damian?"

The names shot through Xavier's head. Pressure was building. These were people he should know. "My brothers?"

The sheriff stood. His knees popped.

Large eyes full of confusion, searching his face. "Elijah is your cousin." She said then lifted her face to the other man. "He already left for his honeymoon. Damian doesn't do crowds or people in any form. He left for his cabin hours ago." Her body shifted, and she leaned closer to him. Honey and wildflowers soothed him. Her warm breath caressed his ear. "Damian is your younger brother. He's back from the Middle East."

Her grip around his wrist tightened, holding him in place. Feeling trapped, he wanted to jerk away from her and run, but he knew she was just holding on to him out of fear and shock. He was free to walk if he wanted, he reminded himself. *He was free.*

"You don't remember them either?"

He shook his head, unable to form any words yet.

"Elijah and you were so close. More like brothers. He was your best friend and business partner. Your father had guardianship of him and Belle. You grew up together." A desperate edge lined each word.

Cantu made his way up the steps. "Belle's inside?"

"Yes, with a few others." Her gaze stayed linked with Xavier's and her hand went back to his face. "You're here.

Right in front of me. How did this happen? Why were we told you were dead?"

His hand rolled into a fist under her hold. Xavier fought the urge to push his forehead against his palm. He didn't know these people. But he couldn't allow himself to show any weakness. His jaw gritted, he stared straight ahead.

"Let me get Belle and send everyone else home." Two steps later, the sheriff stopped. "What about the ki—"

"My dad took all the kids to my house. We were about to clean up. Belle's in the backyard," she replied, her voice sounding stronger.

When the door opened and closed behind the sheriff, he was alone with a wife he didn't remember. Shifting, he pulled out of her reach. If he had any chance of controlling his ability to speak and think, he needed space.

Leaning against the post opposite of her, he looked out into the night, past the lights and into the darkness. In the silence, he could make out the waves hitting the distant shore.

Homesickness was a sucker punch to his gut. It almost knocked him back. Until this moment he hadn't realized how much he had missed the ocean. "The ranch? Does it go to the Gulf?"

She got to her feet but didn't move toward him. "Yes. There's over a mile of coastline. About half is sandy beaches, the other half rocky. How do you not remember?"

"We were ambushed. I was unconscious for a few days. When I came to, I had no memory. I woke up in a hidden camp." His voice was raw and low.

"The rebel group?" She moved closer.

Turning, he tried to study her face. He nodded, and pain shot up his neck, going straight to his eyes.

"None of that matters right now. You're home. It's a miracle." A soft laugh floated in the air. "I don't use that word lightly. But I don't know what else to call it when a man returns home from the dead." Her mouth turned up at the corners. "At Christmastime, no less. My eyes say you're here, but it doesn't seem real." She cupped his face, her thumb smoothing over his cheekbone.

Giving in to the pain, he lowered his body to the steps, dropped his head in his hands. He closed his eyes, but the torturous Christmas joy drove through his lids with each pulse.

Following him, she sat at his side. Her gentle touch was warm on his shoulder. "What's wrong? Can I help?"

He stiffened against the desire to lean into her. "Lights."

Coldness set in as soon as she pulled away. "Oh. Of course. I'm so sorry." And with that she was gone.

Alone, he rubbed hard against his scalp, pushing the pain away. It was stronger than him. He heard the door open, and immediately the lights went dead.

The peaceful light of the moon was a welcome relief and he took in a deep breath. The door closed, and her soft footsteps stopped right behind him. His gaze stayed focused on his boots.

"Is that better?" Her voice was as soft as a summer shower washing away the heat and grime.

He nodded when all he really wanted to do was beg her to hold him. He might not have clear memories of her, but she was somewhere inside him. The need to be close to her had him wanting to share his fears and concerns.

He didn't share with anyone.

Despite his best efforts to keep her at a distance, she settled in next to him. One more inch and she could rest her head on his shoulder. His gut tightened. "We've done this before. Sat on the steps and looked at the stars. You'd rest your head on my shoulder." The memory was like an old photograph, without any sense of time or reason.

One move and she had her head resting on him, her hand flat against his heart. "You remember."

He hated the hushed excitement in the soft voice.

"No. More like a feeling of déjà vu."

The smell of honey and wildflowers surrounded him in the quietness of the night. The scent made him want to bury himself in her hair and hide, but he didn't. The scent was so familiar. More so than his own name. He snorted at the irony of that.

"What is it?" she asked him.

He reached out and touched a strand of hair falling along the side of her face in a long, lazy curl. The rest of her hair, dark and thick, sat in some sort of fancy twist on the top of her head. "I know your scent. Summer Sunshine." He closed his eyes and groaned.

Before the last word was out, he wanted to pull it all back. "That sounded kind of creepy."

"How do you not know me, but you know the name of my shampoo and lotion?"

"I'm not sure. Maybe smell has its own memory bank?"

"It's from a local farm. I've worn it since high school. No matter where you were, each Christmas I'd get a basket full of the soaps, shampoos and lotions, even laundry pods and candles from you."

"I haven't been..." The words stopped. Not a single

found it to his lips. He closed his eyes and gritted his teeth.

She waited but then must have realized he couldn't speak.

"No." She sighed. "I was debating whether to go and buy it myself. It would mean you were really gone. But you must have set it up on an annual thing because I received a box in the mail. The first year I cried like a baby." She sat up and pulled her knees up to her chest. "Receiving the gift was strangely like losing you all over again."

Unshed tears were in her voice, but she wasn't crying. He wanted to make it right but didn't have a clue how to go about doing that.

With a sigh and her face turned to his, she touched the corner of his eye, tracing the scar that went to his jaw. "What do you remember?"

He searched his memory, trying to pull up something, anything, that might make her smile, but it was still blank. "I'm sorry. Until they extracted me from the camp, I thought I was someone else. My brain is a scrambled mess of false information."

She stood and walked to the other side of the steps, gripping the railing. He readied his body to catch her if she fell again. To his relief, she settled in one of the rocking chairs.

"You know my scent, but you don't know who I am?" she repeated.

Xavier didn't say a word. Instead, he studied the night sky. In her voice there was so much hurt. Hurt he had caused. "Now that I'm home, the doctors say I have a good chance of recovering most of my memories. And with therapy, my eyesight could be healed."

"Your eyesight?"

He tapped his fingers against his head. "I had some damage. Brain trauma. My vision was affected." He stopped talking and closed his eyes. "But I know your voice. It's here." He touched his temple. "I just need to sort through the information."

She gasped. "You're blind."

"Not really. More of depth issues and…" He rubbed his forehead. "Words are sometimes hard to form. There's a disconnect from my head to my mouth. It all comes and goes."

Wife. Selena. Yes. Those words he knew. They just needed filing in the right place, connected to the right images. Then he could get his life back.

Carefully, he opened his eyes and tried to explain again. But how could he when he didn't understand it himself?

"Xavier, this is just so overwhelming."

Before he could reply, the door opened. He stood, not wanting to be in a position of weakness. A blur of figures rushed the porch. One didn't stop at the steps but leaped from the porch into his arms.

All four of her limbs wrapped around him. She was crying his name repeatedly, her words coming so fast he couldn't organize them.

But the smell of her was so familiar that tears burned his eyes.

"Belle, sweetheart. Ease up a bit." Selena now stood behind her.

This was his cousin, raised with him as a sibling. She squeezed, silently refusing to let him go. His arms tightened. He had hurt her. This tall woman he had protected since she was a small girl. He had promised to always

be there for her through all the trials they had faced together. To the world she had looked strong and fierce,
but he had known the truth.

She had needed him in ways no one else had.

Was that why he remembered her instead of his own
wife? He took in the front of the house. And then it hit
him.

This was where he had grown up. Memories bombarded his brain, images, sights and sounds ricocheting
and pinging around his mind until he couldn't make any
sense out of them. Pain and anger mixed with laughter.
It was like someone recording as they made a mad dash
through an art museum.

He tried closing his eyes again to block the imagery,
to take control and slow down the flood of memories he
didn't have the time to process.

Belle pulled back and gripped his face. "It is you!
How? I can't believe this."

Selena gently tugged her off him. "He doesn't remember us. Give him some space."

A small sob came from Belle.

Guilt kept him from pointing out he did know Belle.
Not any detailed memories, but he knew who she was
to him.

One more hug and she dropped to her feet. Reluctantly
he let her go. The two women were complete opposites in
stature. Tall and strong, Belle looked more than capable
of running a ranch. He turned to the woman behind her,
his wife. She was the opposite. So small he could imagine she'd break easily.

More people gathered on the porch. He took a step
back. Unable to make out details or faces, he closed his

eyes again. How many of these people was he supposed to know?

Xavier glanced around, uneasy at all the unfamiliar people staring at him. His head was pounding, his stomach upset, his whole body aching. He leaned closer to Belle and lowered his voice. "Is there somewhere more private I could sit down?" He brought his eyes up to his sister's face. "I'm sorry. I just…"

His sight blacked out, his heart raced, and heat suffused his body. All the signs of a panic attack were being checked off. He needed to get somewhere fast.

Soft hands touched his upper arm. Looking down, he fell into the large golden-brown eyes of Selena, his wife. A memory surfaced of sitting across from her in a booth, laughing as she stole food from his basket after claiming not to be hungry. She worried that her tiny hourglass figure would turn into a beach ball.

He had laughed, but his words had never reassured her, so he had let her steal his fries without comment.

Her fingers squeezed his arm, bringing him back to the present. "Do you want to follow me? There's a room in the house we can go."

He wanted to tell her about the memory, but it was too late. His mouth couldn't form a word.

People were talking, asking questions, everyone blended into one giant mob. He reached for her hand, lacing his fingers with hers, and nodded. He followed her blindly through the small crowd as people touched him, greeting him. They all meant to be friendly, but it was too much.

As she opened the door, he heard Sheriff Cantu explaining to everyone that it was time to go home.

Home. Would he find the answers he needed? Would

he ever be whole enough to finish the job he started? He didn't know what that meant yet, but his brain wouldn't let go of the phrase.

Return and finish the job. He didn't know who or what, but he would get it done. That's one thing he knew about himself. He never left a job undone.

He just needed to figure out what the job was and who he was working for. Then he'd go back and take care of business. He closed his eyes to ease the pressure in his skull. One day at a time. First, he needed to heal his body, regain his memories, and then he could go back to Colombia.

Chapter Two

Selena led him deep into the house, where they'd be surrounded by silence instead of curious stares. The office was at the end of the hall, behind the kitchen. She closed the door. "You can open your eyes now, if you want."

Selena dropped his hand and stepped back. And for what seemed like an eternity, they stared at each other. There was so much to say, but all she really wanted to do was look at him. Since she's received the news of his death, a part of her had expected him to show up, walk through the door, back from another secret mission. But everyone told her that was a normal part of grief. What they didn't know about was the guilt.

Especially with the way they had lost him, with no real closure. Just a box of ashes and belongings. It had seemed so surreal, but now he had walked back into her life and it was just as unsettling. "Whose ashes do we have?"

"Pedro Sandoval. They thought I was him and that Xavier De La Rosa had been killed. Our I.D.s had been switched, and I don't know why."

She sat on the edge of the small sofa and pointed to the

chair across from her. He sank into the soft leather. She tried to gather her thoughts. That proved to be impossible.

Raising his head, he took in the room, then shot up from the chair. "I don't want to be in here."

Searching for the door, he spun until he found it. His chest expanded in short, shallow pants and he pressed his forehead to the solid wood.

Selena jumped up and took his hand. When she opened the door, he shut it again.

"There are people out there." His voice was raw.

"It's okay. We'll go across the hall. No one will see us." He nodded, clinging to her fingers.

As her bare feet hit the wood floors, she mentally slapped herself for bringing him into one of the worst places for his memories. She wondered if he remembered clearly what had transpired in this office, or if he merely got a bad feeling being in here. His old room was close by, but it was covered in his nieces' love for pink and horses.

She led him into the girls' bedroom. "This is better, right?"

He dropped her hand and flexed his fingers. "Great, now you think I'm a complete freak."

She couldn't stop a giggle. "You could always find humor at your quirks. This is your old room. Now Belle's girls share it."

He sat on the edge of one of the twin beds, looking a little out of place on the old-fashioned quilt with its blocks of bright pink and purple.

"So my quirks aren't new. Not sure how I feel about that." His eyes turned darker. "Why did that room upset me?"

"Sorry about that." Selena moved the wicker chair from the small white desk closer to the bed. To him. "Did you remember the room?" A catch in her voice warned her she was barely holding on.

He shook his head. "There were shadows reaching for me, pulling me under. A major anxiety attack was hovering, waiting to hijack me." He lowered his head and massaged his temples. "This room doesn't do that. All the pink and purple scares the shadows." He looked up and the crooked grin that melted her heart every single time emerged. That smile had gotten him out of trouble more times than she could count.

Her throat constricted, and she pressed her lips together to stop the sob. She didn't think she'd ever see that smile again.

"I think it's okay if we're confused and overwhelmed."

He scoffed. "That might be an understatement. What was that room?"

"Your father's office. You always hated that room and refused to go in it."

Shaking his head, he pinched the bridge of his nose. "It was like dark clouds were trying to swallow me in there. I couldn't breathe. Memories were fighting against my own brain."

She grimaced. "Sorry. I imagine some of his worst punishments happened in there."

He jerked his head up and sat straight, on high alert. Unspoken horrors flooded his gaze. "My father. Where is he?"

The heaviness of something close to hatred crept into the room. Her skin crawled.

She felt the need to hold him and went to him, taking one hand in both of hers. She savored the feel of his warmth. "I'm sorry." She bit her lips. There was so much to tell him. "He's dead. He died six months ago."

His eyes narrowed, shifting between green and gray. He tilted his chin to the ceiling as if looking for answers. "I should feel *something*, right? Is it wrong that I'm not upset?" Confusion clouded those beautiful eyes. He shook his head. "How?"

"Damian found him on the back five hundred when his horse came in without a rider. Basically, he drank himself to death."

For a while, the room was shrouded in silence. Selena's hand stayed on his forearm. She just wanted to stay here, not push or pull him. Xavier was alive and well. There were so many problems lingering over them, but for now she wanted to forget everything and absorb this marvel of him sitting next to her.

She wanted to live here, in this peace. The man that had held her hand as she grew into a woman was home. Even if everything was different now, she wanted to hold off from reality as long as possible and just be in this bigger-than-life moment.

A sound on the other side of the door jarred her. Xavier shifted so that he was between the door and Selena.

It eased open and Belle stepped through. She moved to the end of the bed, her fingers interlocked in front of her. "Is it okay if I sit next to you? Please?"

The corner of his mouth twitched. "I don't remember you ever asking permission for anything before."

Selena scooted back, dropped contact with him. How could he know so much about his family but not her? "You remember that?"

"It was a guess." He shrugged, then reached out and took Belle's hand, stopping her from moving away from him. "Sorry. Yes, please sit next to me."

The bed squeaked slightly as her weight came down

next to him. Her hands found his, twining their fingers together.

Belle stared at him as if she still couldn't believe he was here, sitting with them. Selena totally understood that.

She glanced at Selena. "We went ahead and cleaned up. I thought y'all might want a little time to yourselves." Her gaze went back to Xavier. "All of the guests have gone home. My girls went with—" Belle shot a questioning look at Selena.

Frantically, she shook her head. Oh, no, she hadn't told him about the triplets. She hoped Belle would get the message. Telling him about the boys was too much tonight.

"Your girls…" Xavier pinched the top of his nose. "Cassie and Lucy?"

Eyes wide, Belle nodded. Raising her hand to touch his cheek, she smiled. "You remember the girls?"

"Just now, when you mentioned them, their names came to me. I was there when they were born."

"You were my birth coach. You and Selena."

How did he know their names but had forgotten hers? Selena bit her lip. Now was not the time to cry, not here in front of them.

"So we were raised together? What about your parents? How—" His words just stopped. He closed his eyes.

"My mother is your aunt. She dumped Elijah and me here when we got in the way. No clue about our fathers. But it doesn't matter. We've always had each other's…" she bit her lip. "And now your back."

Xavier wrapped an arm around her and pressed his forehead to hers. "You were the only thing I remembered from my past."

"They told us that the company you were traveling with was ambushed. Everyone was killed when your vehicle took a direct hit and exploded. So how are you here?" Belle now had both of her hands wrapped around his left one, as if she was afraid he would disappear again if she let go.

Horror filled Selena's brain. Her voice cracked several times as the words came out, one by one. "Should we have come looking for you?"

"No. It wouldn't have made a difference." Xavier tilted his head back. "The only information I have on the timeline of events is the version the authorities gave me, but it still feels like it all happened to someone else."

She could tell he didn't want to talk about it. The strain of stringing the words together took so much from him. She stood and was going to suggest they stop for the night and get some rest, but he spoke.

"At first my brain was a complete blank. When I woke up, I was a hostage in a guerrilla camp."

Belle's fingers tightened around his.

Selena took his other hand in hers. The calloused skin over strong fingers was so familiar. It was as if he had never been gone.

"You've been a hostage for the last two years," Belle whispered.

Selena could hear the harsh emotion in Belle's voice.

He took his hand out of hers and tucked a loose strand of hair behind Belle's ear. "My memories had been confused. I thought they were lying when the authorities told me you were my cousin." He rubbed the back of his neck. "We were raised together? We survived my father?"

Belle's breath caught, as if she was holding back a cry. She nodded. "And you survived Colombia."

He cut his gaze across the room, where several family pictures were thumbtacked to the wall. "Elijah's your brother. Damian's my younger brother. Is there anyone else?"

Selena could tell that Belle was too emotional to talk, so she took over. "There's a much younger sister, Gabby. But you haven't seen or heard from her in years."

With a deep scowl on his face, he leaned back.

Selena reached out a hand and rested it on his arm. "We have time for this later," she said with a catch in her throat.

The boys. She needed to tell him about their sons. But that wasn't news she could just drop now. *Oh, by the way, you have triplets.*

"Selena, I'm so sorry—"

"Shh. We'll talk later."

Since the moment she saw him, her insides had been numb. What if she was dreaming? People didn't return from the dead, not in real life. But the scars on his face and the gauntness were too real. How much weight had he lost?

The haunted shadows in his eyes were the worst thing. He was struggling to remember her.

She gave him space, but her hand rubbed his arm. "It's okay. You don't have to—"

His hand covered hers. Desperation haunted his Spanish-moss eyes.

"I had flashes and images of things that I didn't understand."

He had always been too proud to beg, but he seemed to be on the cusp of falling to his knees and crying.

"It's okay," she whispered. "You don't have to understand tonight." She stroked his hair. "I think this has been a little too much for all of us. You need rest. There are a million questions, but right now I can't organize my thoughts, so I can't imagine what you're going through."

She pushed his hair back from his temple. "When was the last time you ate?"

"I'm sure it hasn't been that long. I don't reme—"

She gave him a look that stopped his words. "If you don't remember, then it's been too long, right? You have something for pain?"

Belle patted his hand. "When I get a headache, a dark room and an ice pack work wonders."

"An ice pack and no light or sound would be great right now." He kept his eyes closed.

"You're home, now you need sleep. We'll talk in the morning." Selena stood and stepped back. "Do you have meds?"

He nodded. "In my backpack. I think I dropped it by the car."

Belle went to the door. "Cantu brought it in. I'll get it for you. I'll get you something to eat, too. Do you need anything else?"

"Just a dark room."

"You might not recognize it with all the pink, but this was your old room. It's Cassie's and Lucy's now."

He moved to stand. "I'm not going to take their—"

"Stop. They're at a sleepover tonight." Belle opened the door. "Tomorrow you'll go home with Selena, but for tonight let me take care of you. I'll fix all your favorite breakfast foods before sending you home with your wife."

Selena forced her lungs to work. Of course, everyone would assume he'd go home with her. That was his house. She rubbed her temples. There had to be another solution.

Belle firmly shut the door behind her, unaware of the seed of panic she had planted in Selena's mind.

"Does anyone ever win an argument with her?" he asked.

Selena snorted and stood. "Nope. Tomorrow will be time enough to plan out where you'll stay." She had until morning to come up with a legit reason he couldn't come home with his wife. No one knew that their marriage had been over.

"I didn't come back for people to take care of me." Low and gravelly, his voice turned her spine to mush. She straightened.

"You can't drive. You can't see, and you can't speak some of the time. Living on your own is not an option right now. And where would you get the money?"

He growled. Actually growled at her.

"I know you don't remember our house or me, but there had been a garage added and you converted it into a man cave. It's right next to the house. You can stay there. Xavier, I'm sorry but—"

"Let's make an agreement not to apologize every time we speak the truth, or the word *sorry* is going to get repetitive and obnoxious." He didn't look very happy. "I have money in an account. It'll take care of any needs I have." His back was straight, his jaw set in a very familiar hard line.

No doubt about it, his pride was still intact.

She wanted to ask him when they started keeping secret accounts. He wouldn't remember anyway.

He sighed. "I hate this."

"We're family, and family takes care of each other. We'll work it out tomorrow." Maybe another solution would come in the light of day. She wasn't sure having him back in her space would be good for any of them.

He rubbed his head again.

"Belle is bringing your meds and some food. Do you want me to turn off the light?"

Nodding, he kept his eyes closed.

After plunging the room into darkness, she turned and rushed out the door. As soon as it closed, she pressed her back to the wall and slid to the floor in the hallway.

Selena wrapped her arms around her middle. The emotions she had been holding in erupted. Her husband had returned from the dead and was home. They'd been granted this incredible, life-altering gift.

But where did that leave them now? Their marriage had fallen apart before he left. It had been over, but with the news of his death she had decided not to follow through with the divorce. She didn't even know where the papers were now.

There had been no point to mess with everyone's memories of him.

She hadn't talked to anyone about their problem. No one knew. Her husband didn't even know.

When they'd gotten married, he'd told her that he would love her forever and that nothing would ever separate them. He'd vowed back then that, even if he lost everything, she would be the one thing he clung to. Apparently, forever had a time limit.

The day he left for the job, the anger had consumed her. In a rage she had gone online and had found the website to start legally ending their marriage. She had wanted the paper in hand when he walked through the door to prove how serious she was about ending his secret work. But he had never walked back into their house.

So much in her life had changed. She had to tell him about the triplets. That would be a shock, even if he had all his memories.

Before he left for the last job, they had gotten another negative result on a pregnancy test. As he had held her, he'd said it might be for the best.

At the time, that had torn her heart in two. They had always been on the same page, but she had drawn into herself, had pushed him out. The love that had burned bright had gone out. They had been left with nothing but ashes.

Now she wasn't even a part of his memories.

She would never forget staring at the door after he left, waiting for him to come back. He hadn't returned. Until now. But it wasn't real. He hadn't returned to her.

There would be no starting over.

She wouldn't think of the past. Instead she chose to focus on the boys. They had their father now.

"Selena." Belle stood in front of her, a duffel bag over her shoulder and a plate of food in one hand. She crouched down. "Sweetheart, are you okay?"

She nodded.

"So, you didn't tell him about the boys?"

Her throat was too tight to speak. She just shook her head.

Dropping the bag and setting the food aside, Belle pulled Selena into her arms. She shifted, leaning against the wall. "We have him back. It's something straight out of a movie. But we're De La Rosas, and we don't do anything the easy way. Not even death or reunions. And, man, his timing. 'Home for Christmas' has a whole new meaning."

Selena couldn't help but snort against the denim jacket Belle had put on over her formal gown. "It's the most amazing gift ever. Belle, I spent the last so much time telling myself that he was gone forever. Now I'm so afraid I'll wake up and find out this is some twisted dream."

"I know. But for Xavier this has to be a nightmare. We don't have a clue what he's been through."

"I should have told him about the boys."

Belle shook her head. "No. It would have been too much. In the morning, after we've all had time to process, we'll talk. This is better. This way, as soon as you tell him, he can meet them. There's no point in telling him now. He already has too much information to process. You did the right thing."

Or had it just been the easier thing? She wriggled out of Belle's embrace and stood. "Let me take this to him. Then I want to go check on my boys."

Understanding and warmth radiated from Belle's deep gray-green eyes, so much like Xavier's. A sob escaped her throat,

She needed to hold her babies and snuggle them, to feel their little heartbeats. They didn't even know their world had just changed.

Four years ago, she'd been too angry at God to trust him with her marriage or anything else. Not leaning on Him had led her to push her husband away. This time she had to stay in her faith. She had to trust God.

One thing was for sure. She couldn't trust her heart or the stranger that the world saw as her husband.

Chapter Three

Yellows and soft pinks marbled the sky as the sun rose from the watery horizon. Selena glanced into the rear-view mirror, checking on the boys out of habit. In the far backseat of the Suburban, her nieces were singing. From the corner of her gaze, she caught her own reflection.

Puffy, bloodshot eyes made it obvious there had been no sleep for her last night. She'd lost track of the hours she and Belle had talked on the phone. Every time one of them had said good-night and promised to go to sleep, the other would call again.

Her phone vibrated and she cast a glance at her father seated beside her. "Dad, would you check that and see if it's someone I need to talk to?" The phone had not stopped for the last few hours. Word had spread that her husband was back from the dead. She wanted to turn it off, but with so much going on, she didn't dare.

Riff glanced at the screen, then shook his head. "Not anyone you need to talk to right now."

"Tía Selena!" Cassie, Belle's older daughter, yelled from the third-row seat. "Lucy and Rosie won't stop singing. I have a headache."

Elijah's six-year-old daughter's eyes went wide, and she clamped her lips closed. Lucy just sang louder.

"Lucy, I love your voice, but it is a bit early. Be nice and wait to sing once we're out of the car."

The tight pressure pushed harder at the front of her skull.

Her father stared at his coffee without taking a sip. "This has to be a crazy dream. How is Xavier back from the dead? Are you sure it's him?" Even though his voice was low, he twisted and looked at the boys, worry on his face. "Oh, I shouldn't say stuff in front of them, but I can't even start…" His voice dropped, and tears hovered in his eyes again.

Riff had loved Xavier from the moment she had introduced them. Other fathers cleaned guns and threatened new boyfriends, but not her dad. No. One look at the young Xavier and her father had wrapped his arms around him and encouraged her to keep that boy around. Then he'd taken off on another tour.

When they'd received word of Xavier's death, her father had come home and hadn't left. She kept expecting to wake up one morning to find him at the door with his bags packed, but for the first time in her life, he had stayed.

Sawyer, Finn and Oliver chattered in the nonsensical language they all seemed to understand completely. Even Oliver, usually the quiet one, was full of energy and giggles today.

It was as if they knew something very important was about to happen.

How was Xavier going to react? Fingers tightening around the leather of the steering wheel, Selena focused back on the road.

She was taking the boys to the ranch to meet— Her stomach heaved, and she couldn't finish the thought. She glanced in the rearview mirror to check the boys. "They don't even understand what it means that their father is dead. Was dead." She blew out a puff of air. "Belle's going to watch them while we talk. The baby goats are in the barn, so they'll keep the children occupied. I thought you'd want to see him before he meets the boys."

Her father shook his head. "What if he doesn't remember me? I'm not sure. Meeting the boys is more important." Lifting his mug, Riff sipped at the hot liquid.

Selena turned west toward the ranch, the sunrise now in her rearview mirror. There was a new day ahead of them. One that she never saw coming.

Her three nieces had fallen quiet in the back, but her boys chattered in the second row. Her father remained silent for the fifteen-minute ride out of town to the ranch. With each inch, Selena's nerves pulled tighter. Xavier was alive. Her babies had their father. Just in time for Christmas. But to her he was a stranger.

Arriving at the house, Selena pulled up to the front porch. Before she cut the engine, Belle rushed out the door.

Glancing to the back of the Suburban, she spoke in a low voice. "I'll take them out to play with the goats while y'all talk. I've been with him all morning. Damian stopped by, but he just left. We decided to wait and tell Elijah on the last day of their honeymoon. This is just so mind-blowing."

Her words whizzed by like bullets as she got Finn out of his car seat.

Selena unbuckled Sawyer as Belle continued. "When you're ready for them, just come on out and they can meet. We haven't told him. He seems a bit overwhelmed. We all do, right?"

Belle bit her lip and wiped her eyes with her free hand, the other balancing Finn on her hip. With a big smile on her face she greeted the kids. "Good morning, gang! Everyone have a good night?"

The kids all greeted her with varying degrees of cheerfulness.

Her father moved around to Selena's side. Oliver hung over his shoulder, giggling. Riff kissed her on the cheek. "I don't think I'm ready to see blankness in his eyes if he doesn't remember me. I'll help with the boys for now." He took Sawyer from her and tossed him over his other shoulder. He kissed her cheek. "I'll give Belle time to tell the girls."

With her father and Belle herding the kids to the barn, Selena headed toward the door. All the hurt and anger that was bubbling up needed to go away. She didn't have time for a meltdown.

Xavier was back from the dead. He was here. He had been her best friend for so many years. Then they had pushed each other away. Maybe she did more of the shoving. Now she had no idea who he was or what he wanted from her.

A million emotions bombarded her. Simple, clear thought was impossible.

Breakfast smells swamped the house. Bacon, toast, cinnamon and coffee filled the air. Belle's go-to when she was stressed was to feed people, so Selena wasn't surprised to see the table piled with food.

Xavier sat with his back to her. His broad shoulders didn't carry the muscles he'd left with three years ago. He'd always been solid and strong.

The healthy, well-muscled husband who had walked out her door for another adventure was gone. It was hard for her brain to recognize this man as the one she'd been told was dead.

When he'd left that last time, she thought her heart couldn't be more broken. But then the news of his death had arrived, and she'd discovered what *broken* really meant.

Guilt made grieving harder. The only thing that had pulled her off the floor had been the three little wonders growing inside her at the time. Wonders who carried the pieces of her shattered heart.

He shifted and turned. Those once marvelous gray-green eyes that all the De La Rosas possessed were faded and flat.

Something wet hit her shirt and she looked down. Tears again? Taking a deep breath, she wiped her eyes and gave the solemn man at the breakfast table a smile.

Solemn. That was a word she would never have used for the Xavier who went to Colombia. He had been in continuous motion, a gleam in his brilliant eyes.

The gleam had disappeared a year before he left, but, too wrapped in her own insecurities, she hadn't noticed the changes in him. They had been a mess. Her forehead knitted in a frown.

With a deep breath, she relaxed her face and gave him her best smile. Well, she tried, but a tight and forced one was the best she could manage for now.

He stood and wiped his hands on his jeans. "Morning, Selena."

"Good morning." So ordinary and normal. The giggles started, and she couldn't stop.

Without a single word, he lifted one eyebrow, silently asking what her problem was.

Every time she tried to speak, the uncontrollable giggles started again. Xavier stared at her like she'd lost her mind. Which was a good possibility. "I'm sorry. I'm just…" And there it went again. "When I'm nervous I…"

He nodded like he understood, but the doubt in his eyes told her he didn't know her the way he used to. With his right hand, he made a gesture to the table. "Belle's made a variety of breakfast foods."

He was polite enough to ignore the ridiculous giggling. "Plus, there's a platter full of what she assures me are my favorites. She and Damian already ate, and there's still enough to feed an army."

She nodded. "My father is here to see you. Do you remember him?"

He shook his head. "I don't think so but seeing him might help. Sorry."

How many wonderful memories were gone?

"So, Damian came down from his hideout to talk with you?" she asked him. "Did seeing him help with the memories?"

His expression shut down. "Some, but not like I hoped."

Remember me. Please. Oh, no. The tears were starting again.

Concern colored his every word. "I'm sorry. I want to help you, but I don't know how."

That was the same problem they had before he left. "No, I'm good. I should be the one offering help to you." She straightened her spine. "No more crying or irrational giggling."

Doubt furrowed his brow.

"I'm okay. I promise," she assured him.

Under his steady gaze, she repeated the words. "I promise."

Now less than ten feet apart, they stared at each other, neither talking. Last night had seemed like a dream, but today, even with all the blinds covering the large kitchen window, she could see him as if he were illuminated. The gauntness, the lines and the scars testified to the hardships he'd endured since he'd walked out her door.

She took a step closer. Should she just blurt out that he had three sons? No. "Are you feeling better this morning?"

With a stiff smile, he nodded. She didn't believe him.

All night she had thought about him being alone, hungry and cold during those years, not knowing if anyone was coming for him. "You were the only one to survive the attack?"

"I'm the only one they took from our caravan, as far as I know. I have zero recall for the actual event or anything leading up to it." He fidgeted with his hands, then shifted his weight and gripped the back of the chair. "Can we sit down?"

"Oh, yes." She went around him to the opposite side of the farm table and sat in a chair. "Sorry. You must be exhausted. You said your sight was damaged. Does it affect your balance?"

Again, a simple nod. His gaze traveled the room, covering every area but where she sat. During the early years, talking had been so easy for them. Then the miscarriage created a shift in their relationship, and each negative pregnancy test had driven them farther apart. Looking back, she knew she had been as much to blame as he was.

Avoiding each other, they'd become strangers living in the same house, but that wasn't even close to the feeling she had now. Now they were true strangers.

They were also parents.

She studied his face, tossing a few words around. *Hey, guess what? You know that whole can't-have-kids thing? Well, our prayers were answered and now you have three sons. Welcome home to a wife you don't remember and babies you didn't know existed.*

It would be nice if they could have one normal conversation first. How exactly did one have normal conversations with someone who had been dead for the last two years? She didn't know, so she asked the first question that came to mind. "So, what do you remember?"

After what seemed like an hour of silence, Xavier cleared his throat. "I can't remember anything leading up to the attack in Colombia. Before that? Everything is fuzzy, mixed with the false memories they beat into me when they thought I was Pedro Sandoval. I don't know which are real and which are made up." He finally looked at her, his eyes desperate as his gaze searched her face.

"I do remember more about you now," he said. "Last night I had a memory about you stealing my fries, but I didn't have the words to tell you."

"Really?" The nervous giggle took over again. She covered her mouth.

"It's all right. I like your giggle. I do have a few images of you. But it's like watching videos of someone else. There are holes. Actually, more like craters." He reached across the table, then moved his hand back.

Little touches used to come so easily and naturally for them. Now she didn't know what to do. Last night was surreal, like a twisted painting out of a dream. Everything in her responded to him. But they were strangers.

She didn't trust that he was here, within reach. "What else do you remember?" She leaned closer.

He grinned. "I had a dream last night. You were wearing a long dress the color of sunset. But not dancing with me." He narrowed his eyes. "By the end of the evening you were mine." He looked down as if searching for something he'd lost.

"That was homecoming our junior year. When you finally got the nerve to ask me out." She leaned forward. "Do you remember our senior prom?"

He hesitated and twisted his lips to the left. "No."

She bit back the disappointment. None of this was going to be easy. Not wanting him to feel guilty, she kept her gaze on the oversize cinnamon roll she had put on her plate. The weight of their silence pushed her shoulders down.

"Tell me," he said. "Maybe it will help."

"We had our first fight on the way to senior prom. You told me you were enlisting. I wanted you to enroll in the local community college with me. Later that night they played one of my favorite oldies, 'Faithfully.' You sang it to me in front of everyone." Then he had promised to never leave her.

He nodded as if he remembered.

"We played it at our wedding." She sat up. Her heart kicked up a notch. Did he remember?

She waited for more, but he kept his head down and the silence lingered. Disappointment pushed hard on her chest. He didn't have any of their memories.

"So…" Looking out the window, he avoided eye contact. "What's the deal with all the Christmas lights?"

He finally turned to her with a half grin. "It's not even Thanksgiving yet."

"I could have Christmas decorations year-round, but no one lets me." She tried to laugh as if she had no worries. "With Elijah and Jazz getting remarried, I thought it would be a great time to pull out all the lights and wreaths." She shrugged. "No Christmas tree or any of that, but the lights. They're my favorite. It just makes everything glittery and enchanted."

He nodded and went back to staring at his food, but not eating. Her fingers curled around a glass of orange juice, Selena fought back the urge to reach out and touch him. "It's okay. You don't have to say anything."

"It's there, somewhere. The first memory I regained was the ranch. After digging I found the location. Nothing fit, so I thought I'd come here and see what I could find out. Belle De La Rosa was the only name I had."

"And you found all of us."

"Yeah. Names are coming to me. I remember my nieces. Belle tells me that Elijah has a daughter."

She bit her lip. *Now. Tell him now.*

Crossing his forearms on the table, he leaned forward. "It's your turn to tell me something. What have you been doing while I was gone? A beautiful woman like you had to be dating once you were single."

For a moment, she froze. "No. No. I was a widow. Not that I had time." Would this man with the blank stare have cared if she had gone on a date? "Now that you're here at the ranch, what are your plans?"

"I have a list of specialists for my eyes and brain issues. I'll find out what's physical and what might be psychological. It's gone untreated so long, but the doctors in Colombia say there's a chance I can regain my sight with therapy. And, now that I'm home, my memory might fully recover, too."

He rolled his shoulders and dropped his head as if all the words had been too much.

"I don't remember anything, but I have this feeling there's a job unfinished in Colombia and I need to complete it as soon as I figure out what it is. I was assigned to protect someone. I don't know who I was working for. There's something missing, and I'm going to find out."

"You never told me anything about your missions. All I knew was you worked for an intense private security company. I didn't even know you were in Colombia until…" She shrugged. "But everyone in your group was killed."

He closed his eyes. "It doesn't stop the fact that I have this driving need to return. There's something compelling me to finish. I can't remember what it was, but I can't rest. I need to heal enough to go back. You don't know anything at all about my last job?"

Her spine stiffened. "Nothing." How could he even think of leaving again? Her mouth opened, but then closed again.

"Tell me about your life while I was…away."

Lifting her head, she made eye contact with her husband, the father of her children. "I'm on the city council now and working with the chamber of commerce to plan a new Christmas event. I run the office for our company, Saltwater Cowboys. Keeping those guys organized is a full-time job. And I help Belle with the paperwork for the ranch." What she wanted to say was that she was keeping his life together for their boys. "With the death of your father, the ownership of the ranch is shaky. I'm not sure how your returning will affect everything."

She was making a mess of this.

"Saltwater Cowboys?"

"It's the business you started with Elijah and a friend Miguel. At first the focus was on charter fishing trips. You added large tourist boats for dolphin watching. They had closed Pier Nineteen, so we bought that property with the goal to restore it. Which we've done successfully." Her throat closed and she bit her lip. The burn in her eyes surprised her. "You'd be so proud of Elijah. It was hard losing you, and I worried about him drinking again, but he's been so strong. It's because of him I've been able to give most of my time to my sons. Our boys."

Head tilted, he blinked. "We have kids? That doesn't sound… I don't remember anything about us having children." His eyes darted across her face, as if he was scanning it for information.

"You didn't know. We made several attempts. When the last one showed a negative result, you decided to take the job in Colombia. A month after you left, I was sick. I thought it was stress. I went in and found out I was pregnant. The first reading had been false. Spotting isn't unusual."

"But you said 'boys.' As in plural. Twins?"

She shook her head. "Triplets. We have three sons, Sawyer, Finn and Oliver. They're twenty-two months old. They'll be two in January. January 19. The last fertility treatment worked." The horror in his eyes burned her and made her want to cry.

She managed a smile. "You're a father."

Chapter Four

He blinked. Her face blurred, and the buzzing grew louder in his head. "Father?" Babies. Three sons. "Where are they?" He stood, but the world tilted. Resting his hands on his knees, he lowered his head and breathed in deep.

Selena jumped up from her chair, but she stopped short of touching him when he held his hand up, palm out. "They're here. Belle and my dad have them in the barn. She has some off-season orphaned baby goats. Your horses are out there, too."

Crossing her arms tightly around her waist, she turned away from him. "Sorry, I'm rambling. All you probably heard was blah, blah, blah, you're a father. Blah, blah, blah."

She paused again.

He waited to see if she had more to say.

"Do you want to see them?"

He straightened and locked his fingers behind his neck, stretching. His sight cleared, and his airway opened. "The horses or the boys?"

In a blur of motion, her head jerked to him. Her eyes narrowed. "That's a joke, right?"

He shrugged. "Not a funny one."

The tension in her shoulders eased visibly. "That was your thing, you know. Telling lame jokes. The more stressful the situation, the lamer the joke." Her bottom lip disappeared between her teeth. "Do you want to meet the boys?"

"You didn't finish your breakfast." This was so much more than he'd bargained for. Getting his brain around the fact that he was the father of three little boys was going to take time.

"Xavier." Cautiously, she moved to stand in front of him, eyeing him as if she was a rabbit and he was the hungry wolf. "Do you want to meet the boys today? If you want to do it another day or—"

"No. Today. Finish your breakfast. Then we'll walk over to…" His throat strangled the next word.

Slender, warm hands touched his. He looked down and stared at the soft, golden skin next to his rough, darker tones. Placing his hand on top of hers, he held it there, never wanting to let her go. How was it possible to be so connected to someone he didn't know?

"It's okay." Her voice was soft and understanding.

More than he deserved.

She went on, not letting silence hover. "You've been gone for their whole lives. They're so little they don't understand. Another day or two won't matter if you want to wait." She pulled her hand out of his grip. "Unless you don't want to see them."

He heard a hint of anger he assumed she was trying to hide from him.

What did he want? To be whole. He wanted to wake

up from this nightmare and be whole. To know who he was without any doubts and shadows.

Studying the beautiful woman that was his wife, he longed to reach out to her, to tell her everything was going to be all right, but he couldn't make that kind of promise.

Hugging herself, she put distance between them. "Is that it? You don't want to meet them. I know they're a surprise."

He cleared his throat. "Finding out I had a wife was a surprise. Learning I have three sons? That's more of a shock."

He hadn't been here for her when she needed him. His gut told him it wasn't the first time.

He held his hand out to help her up. "Tell me their names again."

"Finn, Oliver and Sawyer." For a brief second, her warm touch was his again, but then she pulled away and headed to the door. She popped her knuckles.

"I remember you doing that whenever you were nervous."

Her hands went into her jacket pockets. "You know the strangest things about me."

The hurt in her words made him uncomfortable. She deserved more. "So, we have Finn, Oliver and Sawyer?" He narrowed his eyes, trying to catch a thread of memory. "I know those names."

She nodded. "They're names you picked out. You love classic stories. We'd made a list of boy and girl names. With three boys, I got to use all of your favorites."

As she walked through the door he held open for her, her fragrance, Summer Sunshine, caressed his senses. He wanted to linger. "What would they have been if you'd had girls?"

She gave him a look that said she wasn't happy about something.

"*We* had agreed to Jane, Scarlett and Esmeralda."

Oh. He had used the wrong pronoun. Then he let each name run through his brain. He couldn't stop the horror showing on his face. "I picked those names?"

"No." Her laughter was a bit reluctant, but real. "You only liked Scarlett. That had been our deal. You got to name the boys and I got to name any daughters we had. I did cheat a little. You wanted Sawyer for a girl. Your other boy name was Ulysses." Her nose wrinkled. "But I thought that sounded like an old man's name. Since you weren't here I used Sawyer for our third son."

"Ulysses is retro cool. But Jane? Talk about sounding—"

"We had this discussion already and since you weren't here when I named them I went with those. They were all approved by you one way or another. The children already answer to them. No take-backs on baby names." At the bottom step, she waited for him to follow her.

He brushed past, the sea breeze relaxing him. "I do like Scarlett. If you ever have a girl, then—"

She went rigid. Then she shook her head. "I'm in a good place right now and I don't see myself having more children."

Had he done that to her? He reached for her hand, then dropped his. "Selena, I'm sorry."

How many land mines was he going to trip over? He might not remember most of his life but hurting her took a chunk out of his heart. There had to be a way to get all his memories back.

Flipping her long dark ponytail over her shoulder, she gave him a smile, as if to reassure him, but the light in her amber eyes was out. "Don't be. They're amazing, even though as a single mom, there are days the boys are almost more than I can handle. Not sure what I would have done without my dad. Your family, Belle and Elijah, have been a great support, too."

Her gaze moved back to the horizon and she walked along the gravel drive. "Don't feel sorry for me. Life is good, and God has given me so many gifts." She smiled over her shoulder. "And now it's Christmas."

She bit the corner of her lip. "And you're back. 'I'll Be Home for Christmas' has a deeper meaning now."

A gust of wind played with long strands of her hair. He wanted to pull her close and protect her from the harsh elements. What words could he use to bring the spark back to those gentle eyes? Even without any specific memory, he knew in his gut that she was everything good, solid and joyful in his life.

He didn't know much, but there was a darkness inside him. That same darkness would destroy her light if he let her too close. Was that why he had left her?

Something was wrong, but he didn't know enough to even ask.

Taking his gaze off her, he studied the old barn they were approaching. The wood was weathered gray and the Texas flag painted on the metal roof was faded. It begged for repair. Was the neglect a lack of help or money?

Selena walked backward as she studied him. He knew without touching it that it would be silky as it slid between his fingers.

Her hands deep in her pockets, she had to speak louder to be heard over the wind. "I know things are different and you…well, you're just trying to find out who you are. Maybe there's a reason you forgot us."

This conversation was on a sharp spiral in the wrong direction, but he was saved from responding when she turned and slid open one of the wide doors.

Giggling warmed the air around him. A couple of more steps and the idea of three little people belonging to him would become a reality. Why couldn't he move?

"Xavier?" She tilted her head as she looked at him. She held her hand out to him, concern in her expression. "They don't know you're here. They have no expectations. You can meet them later or we don't have to tell them who you are yet."

A mix of little giggles and adult laughter answered her. He shook his head. Placing his hand on the edge of the door, he forced his body to take another step. A fluttery movement deep in his belly told him to turn and go in the opposite direction.

But this was his family. The life he had forgotten. There would be no putting the pieces together if he continued to run.

One more step and he was inside.

It took a moment for his eyes to adjust to the indoor light. In the center of the barn was a large open area. A thick blanket was spread out and six children were being mobbed by five baby goats. Three girls, older than the boys, sat on the outside with empty bottles—and right smack in the middle were three dark-haired little boys.

A stark coldness started at his core and spread to his limbs. He closed his eyes against the dizziness.

He was disorientated. What had to be a memory rushed through his brain. He stood in the exact same place, but he was seeing different kids in another time.

The children in the flashback were subdued, their giggles quiet as one dirty, matted puppy licked the little girl. She squealed with delight.

"Hush, Belle. He'll hear us," he had warned her.

A lanky boy in worn hand-me-downs that he knew was a young Elijah pulled scraps out of his pocket to feed the dog. She was black with four white paws and a crescent shape between her eyes. She was too young to be away from her mother, but someone had dumped her on the old country road.

Footsteps outside charged his heart into overdrive. He frantically scanned the area for a safe place.

If his father found them with a pup...

"Xavier." The soft plea pulled him back to the current time and place. Selena had his hand in hers. "Are you okay?"

On his left, Belle put her hand on his shoulder.

He looked at her. His blood pressure had to be dangerously high. "We tried to save a stray once. But he found us. The dog..." Did he really want to know what happened?

Tears welled up in his cousin's eyes. "You saved Luna. You hid her in time, but Frank was mad because you weren't in the barn, cleaning."

He remembered now. "But he took it out on you and Elijah." Why did he remember this, but not the details of his life with Selena?

Belle shrugged. "That was the norm for us. But it was so worth it that time. Luna's a great dog. We managed to keep her out of sight for almost a year. She still lives with Selena."

Selena put her hand on his other arm. "You gave her to me. She went on the road with me when I traveled with Dad. When I was in town, you'd come by every day to see her."

Belle laughed as she wiped her face. "I don't think it was Luna he was checking on."

Nodding, he put that bit of past in its place and fixed himself in the present. Blinking to clear his blurred vision didn't help. He could make out the forms of movement, but the details were too vague.

Lowering his lids, he took in deep breaths that expanded his lungs.

Selena's grip tightened, and she leaned in closer. "We can still make an escape." Just being near her made him braver.

Not sure he could form any words, he jerked his head and took a step closer to the circle of kids and goats.

The giggling stopped. Someone stood and moved next to Selena. All Xavier could make out was a thick gray mustache on a man a bit shorter than him, but not by much.

"Xavier, this is my father."

Ignoring the hand Xavier offered, the man pulled him into a bear hug. "Boy, it's so good to see you." Tears were clear in the man's smooth baritone voice.

Blood rushed through Xavier's body. He knew this man. "Riff?"

The man pulled back, his large hands gripping his biceps. "You remember me?"

"Your voice. You taught me to play guitar. We sang together. You like singing."

A robust laugh filled the barn. "Yes. I like singing. Much to my daughter's displeasure." He pulled Xavier back into a tight hug and his fingers dug into his back.

The man was openly crying now. "You're home. Praise God."

Breathing became difficult in the tight embrace.

Selena's hand was on his shoulder. "Dad, I think he needs some space."

The older man stepped back. "Of course. I'm just so overwhelmed to see you here. Alive and well."

His vision cleared. The details of the man's face came into view. His thick black hair was streaked with silver and his amber eyes looked just...

Jerking his gaze to Selena, he opened his mouth, but no words came out.

"Yes. Riff is my father. How do you remember his voice, but not that he's your father-in-law?" She shook her head. "Doesn't matter. You're here to see the boys."

The pint-size crew on the blanket had gotten quiet as they watched the drama unfold. The oldest girl stood, a squirming freckled goat in her arms. "Tío Xavier?"

She looked to her mother for confirmation. Belle nodded and stepped forward. "Your *tío* Xavier is home. Say hi and then we girls will go in the house to get some breakfast while he visits with the boys."

It was like watching someone else. With a sense of detachment, Xavier greeted each of the girls.

First, he hugged Rosemarie. He had no memories of her. She had the same dark curly hair as her mom, but her eyes were the green-gray of the De La Rosas.

Little Lucy rushed him just like her mom. She was a mini-me of her mother and looking at her took Xavier back to the days when he'd sworn to protect Belle and how he had failed. Frank had just been bigger and stronger and meaner.

The last to approach him was Cassie. She was old

enough to have memories of him. He smiled at her. Belle's oldest was tall and lanky and shy. Had he been a good uncle?

An image of holding her on the day she was born rushed him, as if it had happened yesterday. She'd been a week late and he'd laughed and said she'd waited for his return from Kuwait.

A lump formed in his throat. He swallowed it down and looked at Belle. "You got some beautiful girls here. Their father?"

"I hear he's in North Carolina with a new wife." She shrugged and glanced at the girls before lowering her voice. "He hasn't caused any more trouble. Haven't seen or heard from him since the last time you had a talk with him."

He frowned, not liking the sound of that. "Good."

Belle nodded, then taking the girls in hand, she left the barn.

Riff clapped him on the back. "You ready to meet those magnificent boys of yours? You did good." The man laughed. "Course they're my grandsons, so I might be biased, but they're the most awesome little kids you'll ever meet."

"Dad, why don't you grab some breakfast? Belle made her cinnamon rolls and breakfast tacos."

"Of course she did." Riff chuckled, then went down on his knees in front of the boys. "I'm going inside." He glanced up. "You're getting to meet your most awesome daddy."

He stood. "If there's anything you need, let me know. I'll even give up my cinnamon roll." He winked and disappeared out the large barn doors, leaving Xavier alone with his wife and three sons.

Taking a deep breath, Xavier went to the blanket and knelt. He studied the three little people that were looking at him. The goats had full tummies, so they were snuggling up with the boys. There was a little bit of climbing over each other as they settled next to the triplets.

One of the boys, the one farthest from him, with the straight hair, was ignoring the freckled one in front of him. He might not be two yet, but he was staring at Xavier with the intensity of an old man, judging him and finding him lacking.

He would be a hard one to crack. His gaze went to the other two, the ones with identical dark curls framing their faces. It was awe inspiring to look into their faces and see himself. All three had the De La Rosa eyes.

He wanted to reach out and touch the sweet, innocent faces. Pure innocence. How did someone so small, someone he didn't even know existed, take so much of his heart with just one look?

He slipped out of the crouching position and sat on the floor with his legs crossed. A baby goat saw it as an invitation to jump into his lap. But his gaze couldn't leave the three tiny people in front of him. They were so small.

It was a good thing he was already sitting. He didn't think he could stand. "Hello there."

Selena sat down next to him. Other goats climbed into her lap. She picked up a black-and-white kid as she leaned closer to the little boy next to her. "Finn, this is your daddy."

The little boy smiled. "Daddy." He said the word slowly as if trying it out. He lifted a small brown-and-white kid. "Want baby?"

Xavier's heart froze. By the time he thought it would never start again, blood rushed through his limbs. It did it again. His heart started, then stopped, only to rush again. Stop. Rush. Stop. Rush.

Running a hand over Finn's wild curls, Selena leaned down and kissed him on the forehead. Then she nodded to the boy on the other side. "This is Sawyer."

Sawyer gave him a shy grin but scooted a little closer. "Hi. My baby." He lifted a little goat that wiggled into overdrive. The kid turned his head and nudged Sawyer's face. The boy fell back, collapsing with laughter.

Finn didn't hold back and crawled over to him and climbed onto his lap, next to a goat that had already camped out there. He was talking, but Xavier didn't understand a word he was saying. He pointed at his brother. "Sawya ta da go home Mommy say no. No Sawya."

Sawyer stood and moved a bit unsteady over to Xavier. With a very serious expression, he said something to his brother that Xavier couldn't make out.

Xavier reached for the boy. "Is he going to fall?"

Selena laughed. "No. Despite the weaving, he's very sturdy."

The little boy turned to him with a nod and went on to explain something, apparently in a lot of detail.

Xavier looked to Selena for a translation, but a tiny hand gently turned his face so that he was eye to eye with Finn. The toddler was talking again. He said something about Oliver and his mommy.

All else in the world was forgotten. These little humans were part of him. There were no words.

It wasn't that he couldn't get his mouth to connect with his brain. The emotions that swam in his veins left no room for coherent thought. This was different. It wasn't stress related, it was…wonderment.

Finn's lecture came to a stop and Xavier glanced at

the other two boys. Sawyer stood close by, his big eyes blinking as he took in the interaction between his brother and the father they'd just met. With a hug to the tiny goat in his arms, he gave Xavier a friendly smile.

"Thank you, Finn," Xavier told the boy. "I'm very excited about getting to know you and your brothers. Sawyer," he said as he nodded to the other boy, "that's a fine goat you have right there."

Selena pulled Sawyer into her lap. "Oliver, come over and meet your father."

Oliver, the smallest of the three, wasn't having anything to do with him. He made a point to keep his head down, looking at the goat. "That's okay, Oliver. I get it. You don't know me yet. Are you hungry?" He looked at Selena. "Have they eaten yet?"

"Simmon row." Finn took Xavier's hand, but looked back at his brother. "Ollie, go."

For a moment, the world stopped. The tiny hand looked so small in his. The little guy was so trusting. His son. The little guy was his son. The walls closed in and breathing became difficult.

Selena went over to Oliver and took the goat from him. Lifting him to balance on her hip, she held her hand out for Sawyer. "Yes. Your *tía* Belle made cinnamon rolls." Her voice was singsong as she walked to the barn door. She glanced over her shoulder and lifted one eyebrow. "Leave the goat there, Finn. Xavier, please make sure the barn door is closed and secure. We don't want any escapees."

Letting go of his hand, Finn squatted down and kissed the goat on its nose. "Bye, baby." He looked up at Xavier, then strung a long line of nonsensical words together as he pulled him toward the door to follow his mother and brothers.

Xavier hoped Finn and Sawyer had a little more distrust like Oliver when it came to meeting strangers. Surely Selena understood that even a small town like Port Del Mar could be dangerous.

As he picked Finn up, the little tyke touched Xavier's face. "Daddy."

The world tilted and his vision failed. Finn slid down. Xavier grabbed for the boy, but the toddler slipped out of his grasp.

This was the first time he'd completely lost his sight. He opened his mouth to call the boy back, but nothing came out.

Great. His throat wasn't working either. A two-year-old unattended in a barn was not good. Selena had gone ahead. She had trusted him to close the barn and—

His breathing was hard and shallow. It was as if he was being pushed down by heavy waves. Panicking was not going to help.

"Xavier?" Selena had come back. "What's wrong?"

He couldn't see her. He couldn't see anything. He tried telling her, but the words were trapped. Hand making wild motions, he attempted to show her that he'd lost Finn. Spinning on his heels, he waved his arms around the barn. Finn had not made a noise.

Where was he?

"Xavier. Are you unable to talk?"

He nodded, then pointed to his eyes. Using his arms, he pantomimed rocking a baby.

Her hand was on his arm. "Relax. You can't see?"

Closing his eyes, he nodded. He needed to collect himself, before Finn was hurt. He took a deep breath. "Finn."

It sounded harsh and he wasn't sure it was clear at all.

"It's okay. He's with his brothers. They're standing at the door."

His knees hollowed out as the tension fell from his muscles.

She took his hand. "We are going to walk slowly to the house. Will that help you recover?"

The boys chattered around him but Selena never let go of his hand. With each careful step, he regained control of his body. The landscape was blurry, but he could see it now, as well as the boys as they darted between him and their mother.

"Sorry," he said after he cleared his throat. "That's never happened before."

"Do you know what triggered it?"

His son had touched his face and called him Daddy. Instead of confiding in her, he shrugged. "Not sure."

Pausing at the porch steps, she squeezed his hand. "We can wait here a little longer if you need to."

Shaking his head, he pulled his hand out of hers and put distance between them. He wouldn't be weak, especially in front of her and the boys.

Riff, Belle and the girls were settled around the table when they walked in. Everyone except Finn went quiet. Apparently, he had to explain what was going on, who his daddy was and something about babies.

Selena leaned closer to him. "Finn is the self-appointed spokesperson for the boys." Her smile was affectionate as she put the boys in the booster chairs he'd noticed earlier. They lifted their hands to be buckled in as if it was a normal routine.

He caught Belle glancing at him and then away, as if

she didn't know what to say or do. That was oddly reassuring. He didn't know what to say or do either.

Belle reached across the table for a tortilla. "Xavier, there is so much to talk about. With Frank gone, you own part of the ranch now. We'll have to meet with our lawyer and get everything straightened out. There was no will, and the estate is a mess. My mother left twenty years ago, and we have no clue where she is. And there's your baby sister, Gabby. We haven't been able to locate her either." Eyes wide, she looked at Selena. "Are y'all still married? You are, right?" She turned back to Xavier. "Except you're legally dead."

"You'll have to get the death certificate voided." Riff grinned as he added salsa to his breakfast taco. "I've dealt with some crazy stuff, but this is a first."

There was some talk about the ranch, the weather and supplies that needed to be bought. Xavier wanted to join in and contribute, but the pressure was building behind his skull.

The boys were growing restless. Sawyer banged his sippy cup on the tabletop to his own little rhythm. Selena put her hand over it. "Shh. You need to be quiet. Your daddy has a headache."

Riff unbuckled Sawyer. "I'll clean up the boys." He looked across the table to Xavier. "Go ahead and get your stuff so we can head home."

"We can't assume he wants to go with us," Selena said quickly as she glanced at Xavier. "It's all been a little overwhelming."

"Of course, it has been," Riff agreed. "He's back from the dead. I'm sure he's tired and he should be home. Where else would he go?"

Selena's mouth was a little tight. "In his mind he remembers the ranch as his home."

"There's not enough room here and he can't stay in one of the cabins alone. It would be better for his memories if he lives in the home he made with you," Riff argued.

Belle sighed. "He's right about the room. You're always welcome here, but I'm not sure how comfortable you'd be."

"You're going to go to your home, of course," Riff stated. "Why would you stay anywhere else? You come home. We'll be able to help with the doctor appointments and PT."

"Dad, I don't think this is—"

Belle cut her off and turned to Xavier. "You also have to consider that people will think it's weird if you stay here instead of going home with your wife."

Selena glared at her. "I'm not worried about what people think." Her voice was short and tight. "We need to do what's best for Xavier."

Xavier rubbed his temples. "I'm right here and I can make a decision about where I live. I don't want to be a burden."

The one thing he knew was Selena had just seen him at his worst, and he'd rather no one else saw him completely helpless.

After wiping Finn's hands and face, then Oliver's, Selena turned to Xavier. Her voice was gentle and calm, the irritation gone. "I know being dependent on others is difficult for you, but being in town will make doctor appointments easier. Like I said yesterday, there was a garage added on to the house. You converted it into a man cave. That'll give you your own space, but we'll be close enough to help."

The rambling was a sure sign she was nervous. He had imagined getting his own place, but she was right, that wasn't very realistic. Just a few moments ago he was blind and unable to talk. He hated being dependent on others, but until he was fully recovered, he didn't have many options.

"Okay. I'll go to your house."

By the stricken look on her face he must have said something wrong. He pushed his fingers to his temples, rotating them to try to ease the pressure building there.

Riff cleared his throat. "You bought the house and put in a lot of sweat restoring it. You both had a vision for that big Victorian."

He took a couple of breaths. "I need to go outside."

Riff stood in the doorway between the kitchen and family room, gathering the triplets. "Selena, why don't you go with him? Show him some of the ranch. I'll put a movie on for the boys. When you get back, we'll all go home together."

"Is it okay if I go with you?" Selena's voice was low as she asked him. "You don't like being coddled, I know, but I'm worried about you traipsing around by yourself. We can go to the stables and visit your horses."

Pushing back from the table, he gave her a slight nod. He knew that walking alone wasn't the best idea, but he hated that he needed a nanny. She stopped in the family room and told the boys she'd be right back. They were already engrossed in watching colorful characters dancing and singing on the TV screen.

A strange man being introduced as their father didn't faze them, while his world was even more upside down than it had been this morning.

Oh, man. Talk about headache inducing.

He followed her outside, then paused on the steps. The fresh breeze was cool to his senses.

"It's a little humid today."

With a snort, he shook his head. "You don't know humidity until you're stuck in a windowless shed deep in the jungle."

"Oh." Her head went down.

"Sorry. I shouldn't have said that. It upsets you."

She stopped and reached for his upper arm. Her amber eyes sought him, but he kept his gaze on the horizon. "Xavier, look at me. I want you to be able to speak what's on your mind. Holding things in, guarding our words from each other, won't help you recover. Please don't worry about hurting my feelings. I'm stronger than I look, I promise."

For a long moment, they studied at each other, silent. He wanted to pull her close and anchor himself in her sunshine. For all the upheaval of the last month, this felt like home for the first time. She was his peace.

They didn't talk as they made their way along a well-worn path. By the time they made it to the barns, the pressure in his head was gone and his shoulders had lightened. Several horses stuck their heads over their stall doors.

He didn't even have to think about it. Xavier went straight to a dark roan just two stalls down. The gelding tossed his head and talked to him with a low, rumbling nicker.

Selena went into a small room and came back with a bucket of feed. "I see you found Mar Bollo."

He raised an eyebrow. "Seabiscuit in Spanish?"

She laughed. "Yes. Just like the classic characters you pick for kids' names, you like turning famous horses' names into Spanish ones. Bollo here was your favorite. You'd take him out to ride the pastures whenever you needed to de-stress. Y'all would be gone for a few hours. The guy at the end is your newest horse, Hombre de Guerra. He's four now and you call him Hombre. They all have great cattle sense. You were working on cutting skills with them."

He laughed. "Man o' War." He went to each horse. "I want to ride later this week."

"Sure. First we need to talk to all of your doctors and see where you are. What you need to do and what you can do. Once I get you worked into the family calendar we'll see about your appointments."

Still caressing the big gelding's jaw, he watched as she moved along from horse to horse, feeding each one. "Family calendar?"

"With the boys, my city council duties, the ranch and Saltwater Cowboys I have to be super organized or it will fall into total chaos."

She was an amazing woman. Raising the boys, helping the community and her family. She seemed to take it all in stride, even a husband returning from the dead.

Maybe he was too much with her already full life. "Are you sure you're good with me moving into your home?"

She frowned. "It's your home, too. I know we have a lot to work out, but this will give you an opportunity to see the boys and become part of their lives. If that's what you want."

"I came here to fill the holes. You'd be the best person to help me. Since being here, I already have more memories than I had the last two years."

He took a deep breath. There was so much he needed to know that was right out of his reach. "All the memories I'm getting are older, though. Nothing in the last five years or so. If I'm at your house…our house, you can help me sort them. Bring more to the surface."

She nodded. "That makes sense. I know next to nothing about your missions, though. Those were always top secret. Most of the time I didn't even know you were leaving until the day before, and I never knew where you were going."

"So you didn't know why I was in Colombia?"

"I didn't even know you were there until they told us you'd been killed in an attack."

He shifted so he could watch her. Pressing his shoulder against the edge of the stall door, he continued rubbing Bollo, but his attention was all on her. "You do know everything else about me. We grew up together, right? You're from Port Del Mar, too."

He had a strong desire to know everything about her, to know all her secrets.

"My great-grandmother moved here to live with her sister the summer I turned ten. I didn't stay with them until I was a freshman in high school."

He frowned trying to put the new bit of information in place. "I don't understand. I got the impression I knew you my whole life."

"Really? You used to tell me I was the only person who knew the real you." She bit her lip and for a moment the look of longing tore at his heart.

What did he say to that?

"But maybe I really didn't know you at all." She turned away from him.

Without thought, he reached for her. "Selena, my heart tells me you are the only one who can help me put all the pieces back together."

"Then why don't you remember me like you do your family? You remember my father. You even remember the dog." Her eyes glistened, but she blinked the tears back. She had every right to be angry with him. He had let her go long before he had left for Colombia. Now he claimed to need her.

"You don't need me, Xavier. You haven't for a long time."

"I don't understand. Your scent brings me comfort. My instinct is to stay close to you, but since I don't know you, it feels…odd." He dropped his hand and went to the next horse that was trying to get his attention. Dealing with the horses was so much easier.

"I'm all over the place and that's not fair to you." Resting his forehead against the horse's forelock, he closed his eyes.

Summer and sunshine surrounded him. He kept his gaze down and inhaled. Her gentle touch traced his jaw. He looked up and studied her. Saw and absorbed the care and compassion that radiated from her eyes. It was more than he deserved. "How did we first meet?"

Her hand slipped down, and she wrapped her fingers around his. "I was visiting Buelita, my great-grand-mother."

His brows drew in. "Where did you live?"

She shrugged. "All over the country. My father was on tour with a country music band led by a husband-and-wife team. He played the guitar for them and wrote music. I traveled with him and was homeschooled with the lead singers' daughters."

"That sounds like a dream life for any kid."

She dropped her hand and stepped back. She sat on a bench pushed against the wall between two stalls. He wanted to be close to her again, but he focused on the horse.

"That's what you said back then, too. You would have given anything to trade lives with me, but I don't think you would have gone unless you could take Elijah, Belle, Damian and Gabby. You talked about running away all the time, but you never did. Not until you were all grown, anyway."

When she smiled up at him, he took it as an invitation to join her on the bench.

"All I wanted was a forever home that I would never have to leave," she said when he sat beside her. "I envied your life, with your family and the ranch. I didn't really understand your relationship with your father back then. You hid that."

She sighed and leaned closer to him. "The closest I had to a real home was Buelita's house. When she moved in with her sister after Buelito's death, I fell in love with Port Del Mar. One day when I was twelve, some boys were teasing me on the beach. It was early morning and they'd taken my bucket full of shells. You were walking Luna and came to my defense. You walked me home and told me I was too young to go out alone." She laughed. "You were so superior and tall. I thought you had to be at least fifteen. The hero worship started right then."

"How much older am I?"

Gently elbowing him, she shook her head and grinned. "When I asked your age, you informed me that you were twelve, too, but you knew the area, had a dog and were a boy."

He chuckled. "Really? I sound a little arrogant."

"A little? I was so mad. Then you told me that if I

wanted to go exploring on the beach you would take me, and you might be able to find me a dog."

"Did I?"

"Yes. You said that your dad wouldn't let you keep Luna, so I'd be doing you a favor if I took her." She paused. "She's still with us. She moves much slower and does more sitting on the beach then running, but she loves the boys. When I first brought them home, she wouldn't leave their side." This time, a few tears slipped down her face before she could stop them. "It was like you told her to protect them. She always did what you said."

He reached up with his thumb and wiped the tears away. "She's a good dog."

"She is. Do you remember her?"

"I do. She's the puppy I protected from my father. How old is she now?"

"Eighteen. The vet says she's a mix of a couple of long-living breeds. Australian cattle dogs, poodle and terrier. It's not the average but possible. Maybe she was just waiting for your return."

He leaned his head back on the old wood behind him and absorbed all the scents and sounds. The hay, sweet feed, the horses shuffling, and the honey and wildflowers. This was home.

He took her hand.

Eyes closed, he relaxed and let his brain work through all the connections he had with her. "I can see you in the hallway at school." He had wanted them all to know she was his, even if he was a De La Rosa and wasn't good enough for her. She could have had her pick. Had she always chosen him? "When did we start dating?"

She laughed. "Our junior year. You finally asked me. I was texting Belle during a basketball game. She was so mad at you. She told me I needed to set my expectations higher and make you work a little harder."

He faced her. "But you didn't." Lost in the memory of her, he leaned in. "We had our first kiss after the game."

She had been his. He didn't know what he'd done later to drive them apart, but this memory told him she'd been completely his at one time.

Giving her more space, he shoved his hands in the front pocket of the jeans. He might not remember her, but his heart seemed to have other ideas.

Ideas that were not productive at this point.

Chapter Five

Horses shifted in their stalls and the wind blew outside, but the silence between him and Selena screamed at him. He sought for some words to say to break the awkward tension between them, but a sudden noise distracted him. The barn door crashed open and he jumped to his feet, on instant alert. Before he could get a look at him, a man lunged at him and grabbed him in a bear hug.

Elijah, his cousin. His brother. His best friend.

The fight-or-flight instinct receded, and Xavier clung to this man he knew. They'd grown up together when the other man's mother had dumped her two young children with her brother, Frank. They hadn't seen or heard from her since.

They survived their childhood intact because they'd always had each other's back. They had vowed never to perpetuate Frank De La Rosa's legacy of hatred and violence.

Time stopped as memories flooded his brain. Tears streamed down to his neck. He pulled back and turned his head, trying to hide the evidence of his emotional weakness. Selena stood next to him, to let him use her as a shield as he pulled himself back together.

She threw her arms about Elijah. "What are you doing here? You have several more days of honeymoon left."

He hugged her, then looked over her shoulder at Xavier. He gently put her to his side and reached out to grab Xavier's arm. "It's really you." His voice cracked. "When they told me, I couldn't believe it." Elijah pulled him into his arms again. His grip tightened for a moment.

He finally stepped back and pinned Selena with a hot glare. "I'm upset with you. You should have called me right away. Why would I want to be hanging out on a beach when... Xavier's home?"

He turned to his cousin then, tears glistening in his eyes. "Losing you was so hard." He grabbed Xavier's face and looked him in the eye. "I stayed sober and made sure I was there for your boys. You've met them, right? They're little walking wonders. They look so much like you, and Finn is already just as bossy."

Xavier's eyes blinked several times. It was too much.

Selena put a hand on his arm and tried to divert Elijah's attention again, but he wasn't budging. "How did you find out he was here?"

"Are you serious? You know we live in a small town, right? As soon as Xavier showed up at the house, people were messaging me. Jazz and I had turned off our phones. I went to do a quick check and my phone blew up." He narrowed his eyes. "I should have heard from my family." His voice was clipped and hard.

"I'm sorry. We thought it might be overwhelming for Xavier. Plus, you and Jazz deserved your time together."

Xavier stepped up, putting himself between them. "Don't get mad at her."

"We thought you were dead. You're not. She should have—"

Xavier lifted his chin. "Listen. You're here now. I'm here. It's all good."

Elijah nodded and pulled Xavier into another tight hug. "I never got the opportunity to tell you how much I love you."

Xavier's fist gripped the back of Elijah's shirt. He was afraid to say the words. He knew he should, but... he couldn't form them.

A couple more pats on the back and Elijah stepped back, then hugged Selena. "Sorry. It's just so much to take in." He released her and looked at them both. "This is going to be one amazing Christmas. I've never been a big fan, you know. But this year I have Jazz and our daughter. Did you meet Rosie?" His eyes lit up, bright with joy and happiness.

Xavier had a hard knot right in the center of his chest. Elijah deserved happiness.

"I have. She's as beautiful as her mother. I'm so glad you have Jazz back in your life and a daughter."

"Yeah that was a surprise. I'm making up for lost time." Elijah wiped his face. "And now you. I feel like Scrooge when he finally believes. God is so good. We have so much to talk about."

Selena took Xavier's hand. "You know about his memory loss, right?"

The man who had been Xavier's brother and best friend nodded. "Sorry if I came on too strong. Is it rude to ask how much you remember about me?"

"No. When you came in, I got a flood of images and emotions. The last thing I remember is Jazz leaving.

Wait. Once you got sober, we started a fishing charter together." He laughed. "I own a fishing boat?"

Elijah grinned and winked at Selena. "With the help of your wife, you own a bit more than that now. Along with a pirate ship."

"A pirate ship?" He looked at Selena. "Really?"

She nodded. "We haven't gone into all the details yet. There's a lot to work out and go over. We need to meet with a lawyer."

Elijah laughed and hugged them both. "That will all work out. It's like we're in some strange episode of *It's a Wonderful Life*, De La Rosa style."

Selena gave him a quick hug and stepped back with a smile. "It's the best Christmas gift I couldn't have even known to ask for. Will y'all be okay if I go to the house to check on the boys?"

They both nodded, Elijah with much more enthusiasm.

She gave Elijah a kiss on the cheek, then turned to Xavier. "When you're ready to go home, just come get me. Okay?"

He nodded, even though the thought of her leaving him sent a flare of panic through his veins. The horse next to him nudged his shoulder, so he ran his hands under the thick mane instead of reaching for Selena.

Hombre turned to him and Xavier rested his head on the horse's neck. Selena was his home. How did he know that, but nothing about them as a couple?

Chapter Six

The ride from the ranch into town was full of silence. Even her father, normally an easy conversationalist, didn't say much. He cited a few points of interest, but Xavier didn't respond.

She studied him but couldn't figure out what he was thinking. Which was nothing new. He had always kept his emotions tucked away.

The fifteen-minute trip seemed to have lasted over an hour by the time Selena put the car in Park. No one moved. "Well, home again, home again…"

"Jiggity jig," Xavier finished for her, then chuckled. The boys all said their own version of *jiggity jig.* Grinning, he scanned the area. "I have no idea where that came from."

Riff leaned forward and patted him on the shoulder. "Every time I brought Selena home from another tour we would say that. I'm sure it's deep in your rote memory." He opened his door, then unbuckled Oliver.

She watched Xavier's every expression as he climbed out of the SUV and walked up to the house, stopping half-

way. She waited for some sign of recognition. He turned to her, his forehead wrinkled.

"This house is big."

"We bought this almost five years ago for a bargain. You did a lot of work on it and Buelita moved in right before you left on the last mission. A couple months after we were told of your…that you'd been killed, Riff announced his retirement and moved in, right before the boys arrived. We all live here now."

He looked over his shoulder. "I'm glad he was there for you."

They stood shoulder to shoulder, looking at the grand Victorian home with the large wraparound porch that served as another living space. "You can see the beach from the deck upstairs. Whenever you were home, that's where we spent our evenings."

An incessant barking started behind the door. The late-morning light reflected off the cool colors of the stained-glass window. Luna slammed against the door on the inside followed by hard scratching sounds.

Selena rushed to the porch, but before she reached the steps, the door opened a crack and a black dog nose pushed through. A black-and-white blur charged off the porch and launched herself at Xavier.

"Luna!" Selena reached for the old dog who was jumping and bouncing on Xavier like an eager puppy. Her tail was wagging hard enough to propel her off the ground as if she had wings. She licked his right cheek, then the left side of his neck.

Riff laughed as he lifted the last of the triplets out of the SUV. They ran and joined in the play. "Una. Una. Daddy. Daddy."

Selena was having a hard time processing what she

was seeing. "She remembers you. I haven't seen her move like this in years."

Her father had his phone out, recording the reunion. Xavier wrapped his arms around the Australian mix. He rubbed his forehead against the dog's and whispered to her.

The boys jumped into the fray, giggling and laughing at Luna's antics.

With the boys joining them, Luna lay down on her belly, but her tail was still going a mile a minute.

The boys climbed all over her. Xavier scratched her behind the ears like he'd always done. "Good girl." He raised his face to look at Selena. "I remember everything about her. I gave her to you because she needed a home and you needed someone to protect you when I couldn't be there. I told her to take care of you." Leaning down, he cupped Luna's face between his hands. "Good dog." Tears ran down his face and Luna licked them away.

Buelita was making her way slowly down the steps. "Oh, my." She had one hand on her chest and one hand on the railing. "It is you, *mijo*. It's really you."

Xavier stood. He lifted Sawyer off of Luna's back and held him in one arm as he went to Selena's great-grandmother.

The dog stayed right by his side every step, her face upturned so she could keep her eyes on his face. Finn and Oliver went along with them, their tiny hands buried in her coat as they toddled beside her.

"Buelita. I missed you." He kissed her worn and wrinkled cheek.

Her bent fingers cupped his jaw and her dark brown eyes glistened with tears. "I've seen some amazing things

in my life, *mijo*, but this is something even I couldn't imagine. God has brought you home alive."

He covered her hand with his. "There's still a lot that I need to figure out."

She nodded. "You always had a lot to figure out, *mijo*. But no better place than home to do that. Now I've got some freshly fried *papas* just for you and warm tortillas. Beans are almost ready. Come on and sit down. We'll feed you."

"Why does everyone keep on wanting to feed me?"

"You're too skinny, *mijo*. Besides, no one comes into my kitchen without being fed. You know that. Let's get those *papas*."

"Papas. Papas." Beside him, Finn clapped his hands. "Bala."

He balanced Sawyer in front of him as he dropped to his haunches before the boy. "Don't tell Tia Belle that we like Buelita's *papas* better. It would hurt her feelings."

In his arms, Sawyer bounced against him. *"Papas, papas."*

Xavier grinned up to Buelita. "So, your skillet-fried potatoes are a hit with my boys."

With his free hand, he helped the older woman up the steps with Sawyer in his other arm and the dog at his heel. Finn and Oliver followed.

Selena's heart melted. This was the picture of Xavier she had carried in her heart when they were dating.

He had always been a protector. But could he also be the man who stayed, or would he be leaving again? Would the world take him away?

What she really needed to know was whether her heart was strong enough. Could she stand by and keep her heart whole as he walked out?

Her father put his arms around her. "Give him time, sweetheart. It's gonna come together. God brought him home where he can heal."

She wanted to crawl into her father's arms and cry, but she didn't have time for that. He'd never been that type of dad, anyway. He was more "Life is hard, so get back on the horse and ride." But she was tired of playing the tough cowgirl. "He remembers the dog." It sounded so petty when she said it out loud. "I don't understand. I love that he remembers her, but I'm mad, too. Was she more important to him than I was?"

Her father shook his head. "I suspect the dog, us playing music together, Belle, the early years, are all easier for his brain to deal with. I ain't got no fancy degree, but I know a lot about people."

Nodding to the porch, he narrowed his eyes. For a moment he was silent. "That boy has always loved you above all else and I think he knows he hurt you the most with his leaving. If he allows himself to remember that, he's gonna have to remember how much he let you down."

His warmth surrounded her as he pulled her closer. "From the time he was a kid, he took action when he saw something that needed to be fixed. He's one of the most action-orientated men I know, but he couldn't give you what you wanted. Some things are just beyond the man's capabilities."

Taking her hand, he moved toward the house. "He can understand that intellectually, but it doesn't mean he can deal with it. That guilt could well be what's keeping him from those memories."

"Did he talk to you about it?" The hurt tore at her heart.

"No. He didn't talk to me. Or to anyone else, I sus-

pect." On the porch he pulled her into his arms and she rested her head against his chest.

Growing up, she had resented her father putting his music ahead of her desires for a real home. But these last two years he had given it all up for her. "Dad, I couldn't have done this without you. By some miraculous event, my husband is back from the dead. He's home. I should be so happy, and I am, but I also feel more lost than ever."

His arms tightened around her. "Oh, sweetheart. During your growing-up years I was so selfish. But don't let my choices make you afraid to love him."

"It's so much more complicated than that. The bigger issue might be trust, anyway." She sighed and moved away from her father. "We'd better go check on them. Buelita, the boys and Xavier might be a dangerous combo."

"Oh, I'm sure Luna has them all behaving."

She laughed. "That's probably true." She paused at the door. Xavier was home. The last two years she'd had to stop herself expecting him to walk in the door, but now he was here.

The divorce papers were tucked away somewhere, taunting her. What would happen when he did remember their last few conversations? How would the family react when they discovered she had hidden how badly their marriage had fallen apart?

Walking into the foyer, Xavier paused. To the left was a room that looked to be an office, with a desk covered in files and papers. A large quarterly calendar hung on the wall, bright colors highlighting squares.

Toys littered the area rug that lay over the old wood floors. He followed Buelita into a large living room, Luna behind him. Finn was right next to her and Oliver had a grip on her tail. He wanted to slow down and take in the place Selena had made into a home for her family. Four generations lived in this home.

The need to belong here was strong, but he didn't fit. This was the home she had created for her family.

Staying the course, Xavier crossed the threshold into the large open kitchen Buelita had led him to. Stopping, he inhaled the aromas of home.

The spacious room was outdated, and years of use were evident in every worn tile, scratched counter and faded cabinet door, but the love and warmth invited him to come in and sit down.

This was the place of his dreams. On the hot nights in the jungle when the loneliness and heat had been too much, his scrambled brain had brought him here. He hadn't known it was real.

Sawyer tapped his chest, breaking his dream state and bringing him back to the present.

"This is real," he whispered.

"Papas," the toddler repeated. *"Papas."* The word translated to "potatoes" but growing up they had used it to refer to any food.

The corner of his mouth twitched. "You're teaching them right, Buelita. *Papas.* Potatoes. Yummy food." How could he remember her food but not remember the woman he married?

"Papas. Ees papas."

He shook his head. "You can't be hungry after all the food at the ranch." He went to put his son in the high chair that sat at the middle of the long pine table. Sawyer screeched. "No! Ollie's."

Buelita went to the stove to gather the *papas* into a

bowl. She looked over her shoulder at him, as if to say that he should know better. "That's Oliver's chair. Sawyer's is the one on the far right. Finn's is in the middle."

Oliver stood with his hands clasped to the side of the tray, glaring at him.

"Sorry," he said to the serious little guy. "I'll get it figured out." He slid Sawyer into the correct chair, then reached for Oliver, but the smallest brother stepped back. He moved next to Buelita, his chubby arm wrapped around her leg. Her aged hand patted his head.

"This is your daddy. He loves you," she told Oliver in Spanish.

Xavier crouched down, balancing on his heels, and held the boy's steady gaze. Neither of them spoke. His heart was a huge mess. The mixed emotions of being in the kitchen he'd thought was a product of his imagination with three little people that were his had him wound so tight he didn't know what he should do.

He wanted this little boy to trust him, but he wasn't sure he deserved that trust. Finn came over to him and touched his face to get his attention. "Up."

The tightness in his chest loosened a bit as he swung Finn up and slid him into his chair. Buelita scooped the diced potatoes from a large bowl to their trays.

He turned to Oliver, not sure how to proceed.

Selena rescued him. Coming into the room, she went straight to Oliver and placed him in his chair.

Xavier stood back a little. "I can't believe they're eating again."

"They don't really eat much at one sitting, so they kind of nibble on several meals throughout the day."

Riff laughed. "That's what she likes to tell herself. But

these boys eat. I've been saving money for their food bill when they're teenagers."

Xavier's lungs stopped working at the thought of these three babies as huge teenagers. He, Damian and Elijah had always been hungry. There hadn't been enough food to keep them full. Not to mention clothes and shoes.

A warm touch on his arm brought his gaze to the left where Selena was frowning at him. "We have plenty of years yet before we have to deal with that. Let's get them potty trained first."

He nodded. Potty trained. He didn't even begin to have a clue about training two-year-olds.

"I'm going to go get my organizer." She stopped at the doorway. "Do you have a list of the doctors you need to see? I can make calls in the morning and we can set up a rotation to make sure you always have a ride and someone with you. We also need to meet with a lawyer."

"I don't want to be an imposition. You're already busy."

Buelita sat at one end of the long farm table, sorting beans. "No worries, God has us. *Somos familia.*" The tiny lady shook her head at him as she scraped the clean beans off the edge of the table into a bowl.

Selena nodded. "Family is everything. You have always been there for yours."

He looked at the boys, then to the woman that had raised Riff after his parents' death. She was tiny, but had strength radiating from her core. Now she was helping raise Selena's boys. His boys.

His wife's family legacy was the opposite of his. Why had she married him? Maybe she had been too young to know better?

Riff nodded. "Listen to Buelita and your wife. They're

smart women. We are family, so don't you dare worry about being an imposition. You're home. You're alive. Let us take care of you."

"Do you have the list of doctors with you?" Selena asked.

He stood. "I have a folder the hospital in Colombia gave me. No doctor's names, just what kind I need to see."

"Come on, then. That's get this together and I'll show you to your room."

It was like she knew he needed a break from the family togetherness. Back in her office, he studied the shelves and walls while she opened her organizer and wrote down the info from the folder he gave her.

Their life together was scattered around the room in frames. More pictures of the boys hung on the wall. It had only been two years but looking at the tiny babies in one crib made him realize how much he had already missed.

"Here's the plan." She moved to stand in front of her three-month wall calendar. "I'm going to call all the doctors you have listed and get appointments set up. I'll go to the first ones with you. I can ask questions and make sure we have everything covered and what you need for recovery. I'm going to make you…"

She looked down at her cup full of highlighters, then back at the organized squares hanging on the wall. "The boys are my favorite color, turquoise. Everything to do with Saltwater Cowboys is blue." She twisted to look at him. "That's the business we own with Elijah and Miguel. City business is red. The ranch is yellow. Family is orange. Church is purple, and all the Christmas deadlines and appointments are highlighted in green."

Holding up the bright pink pen, she smirked at him. "You always looked good in pink."

He grinned. "Real men wear pink, right?" Then he looked back at the wall. "What about you?"

She gave him a blank look. "Me? What do you mean? All these colors are me."

"No. These are all the people in your life." He pointed to the oversize calendar. "When do you have time for yourself?" His memories were good, but he couldn't imagine seeing anyone so well organized.

Rolling her eyes, she put the cup back on her desk. "Now you sound like Belle. I love my life. All I ever wanted was to be a part of a big family and involved in my hometown."

He looked back at the calendar. "Well, you achieved that goal. You are definitely involved. Out of curiosity, when did we spend time together? Did we have a color?"

The sarcastic remark that popped into her head was bitten back. "You had your missions that kept you busy and I had mine. I tended to stay local. You had a bigger, more global calling." She shrugged. "I didn't have this system when you were here. I was elected to the city council right before you left. A system was needed to make sure I didn't miss anything. And to help me keep the boys in focus. If the turquoise gets overpowered, I know to readjust. My boys always come first." The last sentence was delivered with a verbal punch.

"Selena, I wasn't judging your parenting. You do a lot for other people. I was just wondering what you do for yourself. And now you've added me." He nodded to her massive to-do list. "One more item on your list of jobs. I don't want to be a burden."

"Oh, Xavier. You're an amazing gift from God. A gift that I don't want to take for granted. Buelita was right when she said not to worry. You're family. Taking care of each other is what we do." Her cheeks puffed out as she studied her calendar. "There's not a great deal of wiggle room." She turned to him with a smile. "But don't worry. We'll get it worked out. Your healing has to be a priority."

He glanced at the wall of color coding. "I don't like this feeling of—"

"Not being the one to take care of others?" She took his hand. "Let us take care of you. We have all missed you so much. You being back is like an answered prayer we weren't allowed to pray for."

He nodded. If he spoke, his voice would crack.

Her fingers tightened for a brief moment, then released him. "It's okay to be frustrated. It has to be okay for you to be honest about what you're going through, your feelings."

He laughed. "I have enough of my memories to know I'm not good with those..." He waved his fingers around. "Feeling things. I'm—"

"A De La Rosa. Yes. I've heard that excuse before. If Elijah could manage to find his, you can, too." She let his hand slip from hers. "Get your bag and follow me to your room. They added the garage about twenty years ago, then you converted it. It still has your oversize TV and that giant sleeper sofa. You'll have your own bathroom. You also installed a little kitchenette area with a minifridge and microwave. It's stocked with your favorite drinks. My dad did that. It's like a well-equipped bachelor pad."

Except that he wasn't a bachelor and if they married as young as those pictures looked, he never had been. As they walked through the living room, he noticed the safety gate at the bottom of the steps. He was sure those hadn't been there the last time he'd lived here. "I'm not a bachelor."

"No, I guess not." She opened the door that led to a small passage connecting the garage to the house. She waited for him to walk in first. "Some of your stuff is upstairs in the attic. I donated most of your things to the shelter, but I might still have a few of your shirts and all-weather jackets. Make a list of anything you need. Get some sleep." She went to a closet and came back with bedding and a pillow. "Is there anything else you need from me right now?"

How about a clue to what I'm supposed to do next with my life? But his gut told him a man never asked for that kind of help. "I'm good. Thank you."

"Okay. I'll come check on you when it's dinnertime." She stood in the doorway as if waiting for him to say or do something more, but he wasn't sure what she was expecting.

"Okay. Thanks." *Man, that was lame.*

With a nod, she was gone, and he was alone in the large room that he had designed and decorated. He had absolutely no memory of this space.

Without even bothering with the bedding, he flopped onto the couch and closed his eyes. This big old house was his. He was a father, a husband. With no connection. This was his hometown—where everyone knew him better than he knew himself.

Chapter Seven

The following week had been full of doctors' appointments, strange faces of people he was supposed to know, and getting to see the marvelous world of the three little boys that were his sons.

One afternoon had been taken up in a lawyer's office going through paperwork. His father hadn't left a will, but half of everything already belonged to Belle and Elijah's biological mother—his aunt—and no one could find her. The other half was to be split between him, his brother, Damian, and their little sister. They weren't able to locate her either.

When he had extra time and his sight was behaving, he started doing internet searches for them.

Xavier had also spent more time with family, but after the rush of early memories his brain had decided to lock down any useful information that might help him figure out who he was supposed to be.

Selena's well-organized calendar exploded with pink. A few times he thought she was going to have a meltdown, but she did a great job of covering up and smiling.

Today had been all about Elijah and Miguel showing

him the additions to their tourist-based business. Not that he had much memory of Saltwater Cowboys before he'd left for Colombia.

After touring the buildings and pier and meeting the staff, Elijah and Miguel introduced him to Carlos, the captain of their pirate ship.

A pirate ship. He owned a pirate ship. For some reason he was sure that even if his memories weren't playing hide-and-seek, he would find this hard to believe. The fishing boats fit in a few holes in his brain, but a pirate ship?

Carlos took them through the most notable features of the vessel. Now Xavier stood behind the wheel, looking over the horizon. The clear blue sky was disrupted by white wiggly worms swimming before him.

He was sure no one else saw them. Closing his eyes against the sight didn't help. The little creatures didn't go away.

As the boat swayed, he gripped the rail. *Not now.* Was it too much to ask to spend one day doing things he used to do? Why was it that the biggest battle he waged was against his own body?

Opening his eyes, he found the other two men studying him with concern. He wanted to snarl at them, but that wouldn't help. "How did we become pirates?"

The men laughed. Elijah shook his head. "It was your wife's idea. She thought we needed more than dolphin watching for kids and families and argued it was something the locals might enjoy, too. We had our doubts, but once again she was proven right."

Miguel looked at his watch. "They have a party boarding, and we need to head out if we're going to get any fishing done."

The dock rolled under his feet as they made their way to the fishing boat. It was a beauty but as they boarded, he knew he was going to be sick.

The worms moved faster and multiplied. His sight was useless. The tension coiled, and he wanted to slam his fist into something, anything.

"Xavier?" Elijah was at his side, a hand on his shoulder.

He shook his head. "I can't. The motion of the water is too much. I need to get off the water." He turned to leave, but Elijah stopped him.

"Whoa. You're about to step off the edge." A large hand was on the back of Xavier's shoulder. "This way. Okay?"

Screaming "no" would be childish, Xavier knew this. Locking his jaw, he closed his eyes and focused on the silent directions Elijah gave him.

"Hey, Miguel!" His cousin yelled at their business partner. "Something came up. We have to head out. Catch you later."

"Do you need my help with anything?"

"Nope. We're good."

Yeah, hunky-dory. Like a little kid he had to be led to safety. "You don't have to leave on my account. Just get me on solid ground and I'll—"

"Stop right there. We're *familia* and this is what we do."

Someone was approaching them. He squinted but couldn't make out the details.

"Xavier!" The woman went in for a hug. He stiffened, but she didn't seem to notice. "It's so amazing. God is amazing, right?"

"He really is, Barbra." Elijah said as he took the woman's hand and subtly pulled her away from Xavier.

Breathing became a little easier.

"We so missed the big Thanksgiving Selena and Riff have been hosting at y'all's Victorian, but we understand. It must be just so amazing to be home again."

He nodded and hoped the expression he made looked enough like a smile. She chatted enthusiastically a bit before Elijah finally extracted them from her grasp.

Yesterday had been Thanksgiving and apparently the quiet family dinner at the ranch had not been the plan.

Several more people stopped them. His eyesight was improving, but he still had no clue who he and his cousin were talking to. Elijah charmed them and then sent them on their way before Xavier even had to utter a word. They each said something about the big dinner.

"Did we always host a community Thanksgiving?" he asked Elijah as they made their way to the parking lot. His vision had finally come back.

Elijah shook his head. "No. Selena started that the first year without you. When you left that last time, she got more involved in community service. When we got the news that you had been killed..." He sighed. "She went into overdrive. I think it was a way to distract herself from the fact that you wouldn't be coming back."

As they walked to the parking lot, more people came up to him, asking if he remembered them.

It took them more than twenty minutes to get from the patio of the Painted Dolphin to Elijah's truck.

"I wish I had the excuse of a brain injury to not know people's names," Elijah said as he drove them back to the Victorian. "People come up to me all the time and start talking like I know them. I have to pretend I have a clue who they are."

"It's not as fun as it sounds."

"Sorry. I guess that's true. I have some memory loss related to the years I was drinking. It's really awkward when people remember you doing something and you have no recollection of the event. I'm stuck having to take their word for it and hoping I wasn't a complete idiot. I wonder if I met them when I was drunk or I just forgot them."

"Why not just ask them?"

He laughed. "That would be admitting I'm not perfect. Come on, we're De La Rosas. Not permissible." He sighed as the truck came to a stop in front of the grand Victorian. "It's easier to just smile and nod. Usually Jazz or Belle can tell me later how I know them. I've gotten better in the arena of asking for help."

He slipped his keys into his jacket and looked straight at Xavier. "Just so you know, asking for help is not the end of the world. It can actually make life better."

Xavier nodded. "Duly noted."

Out of the truck, he cut across the front lawn. There were several cars parked in the drive and in front of the house.

"It's annual *tamale* day for our family. One reason I thought it would be a good time to go out on the boat and give you an update on our business." He grinned at him, and Xavier saw flashes of the boy he had been. "We could go to the ranch and ride out to Damian's cabin. He might have his memories, but I'm thinking he's the most messed up out of all the De La Rosa men—and that is saying a great deal."

Xavier considered the offer to run and hide. A black nose pushed a curtain aside and a bark welcomed him home.

They went into the house. "We should offer to help." Xavier patted Luna as she walked beside him. "Maybe they'll turn us down and we can hide in my man cave. Find a football game or something. I haven't seen one of those in a good while."

"That, my brother, is wishful thinking." Elijah clapped him on the back as he went to the door. "It's not that bad. We both have a lot of making up to do."

Xavier was still unsure of how he felt. There had been a part of him that thought he was better because he hadn't turned to alcohol like his father and Elijah. But the bigger the ego, the bigger the fall.

Luna pressed her nose against his hand, and muscles he hadn't been aware of tensing relaxed.

The ugly truth was that he wasn't any better. He was just as much a coward. He didn't hide in the bottle. He actually ran and hid. Using the military and then this new security job, whatever it was, it took him form home. Calling it *duty* didn't make it any better.

Christmas music and giggles floated from the back of the house. Elijah looked over his shoulder with a grin. "Sounds like they're well on their way to Christmas cheer." He paused. "How are you and Selena doing?"

He hesitated, not sure what was safe to say. Or even what he should say.

"It has to be a bit awkward," Elijah continued. "There was always a strange period of readjustment when you got home from a long deployment. This has to be a doozy. Are y'all...finding your way back?"

The psychiatrist had encouraged him to talk to someone he could trust. If he couldn't trust Elijah, he was a lost cause. "We aren't. I don't have any solid memories of her and our marriage."

He looked startled. "Really? Are you talking about it with her?"

Xavier snorted. "I tend to say the wrong thing and make her sad. Not knowing our past is…not easy. I don't have anything helpful to say."

"You have to open up and be honest with her."

"So basically, all I have to do is look like an idiot. Then I can watch her run away as fast as she can. No one wants me to open up, trust me on this."

Elijah pivoted in the entryway, pinning him with a hard glare. "This isn't a joke. If you can't, then don't. Don't lead her on and pretend you can make this work. If you can't give her everything, then at least be honest enough to tell her that and walk away now. Maybe you should stay at the ranch."

Being warned off Selena didn't sit well. Why? He wasn't sure.

He stepped into Elijah's space. "I can't walk away. We have three sons. I won't walk out on them. I will not be my—" His throat closed, and he couldn't get the hated word out. His vision blurred.

Elijah put a reassuring hand on Xavier's tense shoulder. "I know you're not your father. You pulled me out of the gutter when most people would have turned their back on me. You would never abandon your children. Or anyone that needs you. That's part of your problem. But you don't have to be married to their mother to be a part of their lives. There are options. I'm telling you, brother to brother, be careful with her heart. You broke it once."

"Because I left? What happened between us?" Not

having answers to any important part of his life was eating at his gut.

"Neither one of you talked to anyone that I know of, but after you left that last time it was different. She was a hollow shell of herself." He gripped Xavier's shoulder tighter. "You were my role model for what it meant to be a man of honor. I remember your love for her even if you don't, but you need to trust her, too. She deserves the whole man, not the half you're willing to share. She's strong. I don't know what is going on between you, but you have to trust God. Believe me, I understand how hard it is."

"I don't know who I am."

"God knows you." He pulled a piece of paper out of his pocket. "I start every day turning it over to God. I don't leave our bedroom until I've read my devotional and focused my mind. Maybe today's prayer was meant for you."

Xavier looked at the slip of paper. Elijah's handwriting dashed across the page.

Trust in the LORD with all thine heart; and lean not unto thine own understanding. In all thy ways acknowledge Him, and He shall direct thy paths. Proverbs 3:5-6

"Elijah? Xavier?" Jazz poked her head around the corner. "I thought I heard my favorite voices. What are y'all doing back so soon?"

"Waves and head injuries don't go well together."

Jazmine came into the living room wearing a pink-striped, ruffled apron. Wrapping an arm around her husband, she pulled him close and smiled at Xavier. "That means you can help make the family traditional tamales. Or I guess you can go watch some boring game."

Elijah kissed her on the top of her head. "We were on our way to the kitchen."

"Good." She disappeared back out the door.

"Elijah, I'm so proud of you. Seeing you with Jazz—" The emotions welling up in his throat caught him off guard. "Well, it's a good thing to see. You deserve happiness."

"So do you. More than any of us. Growing up, you took hits meant for me. Time and time again, you stepped in to fight for someone smaller."

"Doing the right thing doesn't mean I deserve more than others. There are a bunch of people that step up and do the right thing."

"Do you plan on staying? Selena needs to know where you stand."

"There's so much unknown. I'm trying to get my life together."

"Aren't we all. One day at a time." Slapping him on the back, Elijah jerked his head toward the kitchen. "For now, let's make some tamales with our families."

Following Elijah to the back of the house, the sound of "We Wish You a Merry Christmas" made him want to go the other direction, but then the giggles drowned it out.

He took a deep breath, making sure to plant a smile on his face and breathe.

The kitchen was busy with controlled chaos. His sons had their baby curls in an assortment of colorful hair clips. He was afraid to ask questions.

Buelita held court at one end of the large farm table that served as the island anchoring all the activities in the oversize country kitchen. The woman who had seen nine decades was spreading masa onto the corn husks and then flipping them—all in one fluid motion and without looking down. She made the tricky job look easy.

Standing at her right hand, Cassie was mimicking her, but a lot more slowly. Jazz, Rosie, Belle and Lucy were filling the tamales, then passing them to Selena and the boys to add cheese. Selena, the final stage in the assembly line, was helping the boys and wrapping the tamales.

Hopping off her chair, Rosie ran to Elijah and hugged him. "We're helping Buelita and Tía Selena make tamales! There's chicken with pork and now we're making bean and cheese. It's a family tradition."

The boys tried to escape their high chairs, but Selena had them secured.

Buelita smiled. *"Bienvenido. Como estan?"*

Elijah went around and kissed her on the right cheek. *"Muy bien.* God is good."

Xavier greeted her from the left. "Good. *Gracias."*

She waved them next to the triplets. "Come in. Come in. Now, Rosie, get back to your station. Elijah and Xavier, come here next to Selena and wrap and stack the tamales. Selena and the boys are adding the *queso."*

"Daddy! Daddy!" The boys banged on their high-chair trays.

Selena looked a little frazzled but smiled. "The boys are making what should have been the easiest job much more complicated." She nodded. "I've fallen behind, so if y'all could fold the husks and place them in the red tub, it would be much appreciated."

"Not without putting their hair up," Cassie informed them.

"We all have ponytails. See?" Rosie tossed her head to show off the wild curls gathered on the top of her head.

The boys proudly wiggled their heads and giggled when their short little ponytails and hair clips flopped around.

"So that's why my sons have such fancy hairstyles."

Elijah pulled his well-worn baseball cap out of his back pocket and put it on backward. "Will this work?" He looked to Buelita for approval. She nodded and they all turned to Xavier.

"I don't have a hat. I can go—"

Buelita shook her head. Her grin didn't have him fooled. She loved the thought of him matching the boys.

Lucy held up a glittery purple bow.

"Ponytail. Ponytail," the children started chanting. The boys sounded more like "onyail."

Sawyer grinned at him and pointed to his head. "Pwetty ha." His baby curls were pulled into two short pigtails shooting off the top of his head like fountains.

Selena moved toward him. "Your hair is longer than I've ever seen it." Her fingers caressed the ends that curled behind his ear. "You've always kept it military short. Do you want me to cut it later?"

For a moment, it seemed as if everyone in the room disappeared and he savored her touch. "You used to cut it for me?"

As if realizing she was touching him, she pulled back and locked her fingers together. "I did."

He wanted her to offer to cut it again, but that probably crossed a line. They stood like that, just staring at each other. He searched her eyes.

Elijah coughed, and elbowed him. The moment was broken. "Rigo still has his barbershop on the boardwalk."

"Come here." She motioned to a chair by the small table against the wall. When he sat, she ran her fingers through his hair, pulling it up into the shortest man bun ever. Elijah laughed and took a picture.

"You're so pretty." He smirked. "Damian will want to see this. He might even smile."

Making a point to look at Selena, Xavier said, "I've read that ignoring bad behavior is good practice when dealing with juveniles and toddlers."

"And grown men acting as such?"

Elijah just laughed as he tucked his phone into his pocket.

The kids cheered as Xavier posed for them. He rubbed the boys' heads. "Have they ever had a haircut?"

Haircut and hands washed, the assembly line was back in motion. Selena frowned. "They're just babies."

"You've never cut their hair, really?"

"No. Once those baby curls are cut, they won't grow back."

Belle nodded. "One more step to growing up. The girls were four before I cut their hair."

He looked at the already long curls on Finn and Sawyer. Oliver's was straight, but just as long. "Let me take them with me to Rigo. We'll have a man's day out. Trim up the locks and show 'em how to shave."

Her scowl warned him this was no joking matter to her. "Xavier, they can't shave."

Elijah laughed as he stacked his wrapped tamales. "He's messing with you, Selena."

Her amber eyes glowed, a flame burned hot. "I'm not ready for them to lose their baby curls or to shave. I mean, I know you're not really going to have them shaved, but the idea that one day they'll need…" She bit her lips.

Would he be here when that happened?

Xavier put down the tamale and touched her arm. "Selena, I won't take them if you don't want me to."

Standing next to the boys, she kissed Oliver on the head. "I'm just not used to others making those kinds of decisions about the boys. I'm being silly. You're right. It's time to cut their hair." She stroked her fingers along the silky strands of Oliver's funny little ponytail. She looked like she was going to cry. Making her sad seemed to be his special talent.

With a chuckle, Elijah elbowed him. "You should get that recorded. Her admitting you're right might never happen again."

Jazz threw a small chunk of masa at her husband. "I can't believe you said that."

He dodged. "Not you." With a gleam in his eyes, he rolled some of his own masa. "I was—"

"Children. You're setting a bad example. Ya. Ya." Buelita's glare swept the table.

Everyone went back to work, singing along as "O Christmas Tree" came on.

Selena kept the boys entertained as she added the cheese. Smiles and laughter floated around the kitchen.

This wasn't a one-time thing. For his boys, this was family life, a safe place where they could grow and explore the world around them without fear or doubt.

Elijah reached across and helped his daughter with her tamale. He had the natural ease of a man who knew the value and worth of the people in his life. Xavier had prayed for Elijah, and Belle and Damian and Gabby, to have this. Back when he'd believed his mother when she said God was listening. Then she was gone, dead, and he stopped believing.

But in the jungle, he had instinctively reached out

to God. God had never left him. Even though he hadn't known who he was, God did, and He was here now, in this kitchen.

Xavier's heart pounded.

Their sons were surrounded by a loving family. Selena had created this without any help from him. Maybe because he hadn't been here to get in her way.

His father was in his blood. What if he destroyed this safe haven she had built for her family?

Finn slammed his hands flat against the tray and bits of masa went flying. Specks landed in Selena's hair.

"Finn. No."

Sawyer banged on his tray. "No. No, no. Finn. No."

Oliver pressed his face against the tray and licked the surface.

"Don't do that, Oliver," Selena scolded. "Stop licking your tray." He giggled and did it again. This time, his brothers licked the surface of their trays, too. She sighed in defeat.

Xavier tilted his head and studied the boys. "What are they doing?"

"I have no idea, but once one of them does it, the other two will follow." Going to the sink, she ran a towel under the water. "I think the boys hit their tamale-making limit. I'm going to take them to their room. It's past nap time." She wiped down the one closest to her. "Ready for *mimis*?"

That word hit him hard. A clear memory of his baby sister holding his hand and asking for him to go *mimis* with her. It was baby talk for "sleeping." Gabby had used it well past her toddler years. She'd been afraid of going to sleep unless one of her big brothers stayed with her.

"No. No *mimis*." Sawyer frowned.

Oliver yawned. *"Mimis."*

"Will y'all be okay without me?" she asked Buelita.

"Sí. Sí. We have this. Take your boys." She looked at the triplets. *"Muy buen."*

"Let me help." Xavier dropped his last tamale into the tub.

Shaking her head, Selena turned away from him. "Stay and help with the tamales."

Xavier looked to the mess on the counter, then to Selena. She went to Finn and unbuckled his seat, so Xavier went to Sawyer.

"It's okay. I've got the boys. I'm used to this." Putting Finn on the ground, she moved to Oliver. "Really, Xavier. Help with the tamales. I've got the boys."

She took Sawyer from him and walked to the door. Oliver followed, but Finn took off in the opposite direction. *"No mimis."*

"Belle, would you mind getting him?"

"I've got him." Xavier dropped his last tamale into the tub and went after Finn.

She sighed and held out her free hand. "I can carry him upstairs."

"No." Finn arched his back and screamed. *"No mimis."*

"I can take him up."

"He does this all the time. Just hand him to me." Her jaw was flexing.

Why wouldn't she let him help? He glanced at the others. All the adults were trying very hard to be busy with the work at hand. The kids stared at him with curiosity, waiting to see what he would do.

"You've got three of them. Let me help." Not letting her say no again, he threw Finn over his shoulder fireman style and patted his padded bottom. The boy went from screeching to giggling. "Lead the way, Mama Bear."

She rolled her eyes but didn't offer any more arguments. Unlatching the safety gate at the bottom of the stairs with one hand, she called Oliver back to her. He shook his head and ran across the room to the couch.

"Oliver, come over here."

He shook his head and climbed onto the large L-shaped sofa. He struggled a bit, but finally pulled himself up. *"Mimis."* He pulled one of the overstuffed cushions down and threw himself on it. Laughing, he did it again.

Not able to hold back his smile, Xavier went over to scoop up the smallest triplet. The boy scurried over the cushions and onto the back of the sofa. "No!" he yelled at Xavier. Then he fell off the back of the couch with a hard thunk.

Xavier's heart stopped. Before he could respond, Selena was behind the sofa and picking Oliver up with her free hand, Sawyer balanced on her opposite hip.

After she'd determined Oliver hadn't injured himself, she glared at Xavier as if he had caused the child to fall. He wanted to defend himself, but it was probably his fault. He followed her to the stairs.

In his arms, Finn started crying. Xavier lifted him over his head and made zooming sounds as he pretended Finn was an airplane.

The crying stopped, and Xavier lowered him.

"Zoom. Zoom. More." Finn bounced against him.

Laughing, he lifted the boy up in the air and rushed up the stairs, dipping him over the banister when they reached the top.

Sawyer clapped. "Zoom. Zoom. Me!"

"Xavier. I need them to calm down or they'll never go to sleep," Selena commanded as she put a safety gate in place.

He brought Finn against his chest. "Sorry."

Pushing on him, Finn protested. "*No mimis.* Zoom. Zoom."

Selena shook her head. "Their room is this way." She turned to the left.

He hadn't been up here. At least, he didn't have any memories of it. He stopped and looked around.

Straight ahead at the top of the stairs was a cozy reading nook with a ton of pillows in the window seat. Two floral armchairs sat opposite a tidy desk. Drapes were pulled back on the French doors leading to the balcony.

The space around the banister was open to the floor below. There were two closed doors on the right and two to the left with one at the back. Selena had disappeared behind the door to the left.

"Xavier." She poked her head out the door. "What are you doing?"

"Just getting my bearings. The balcony is through those doors, right?"

She bit her lip and nodded. "Sorry, I hadn't thought about your memories up here. Do you want to go to the balcony? We spent a lot of time there."

"Zoom. Zoom." Finn pushed on him.

"Zoom. Zoom." Sawyer did the same to her.

He laughed at her expression.

"Don't encourage them. No zoom, zoom." She went back into their room.

"Come on. You heard your mom. Time for bed." Xavier bit back a smile as Finn's bottom lip stuck out. "I've seen that look before."

The image of a young Selena danced in his brain. She had wanted something… What was it? He closed his eyes to let the memory float to the surface. The therapist he was seeing had given him a few strategies to help reclaim memories. According to him, there was a good chance they were still there, just locked away.

But nothing surfaced.

Inside the boys' room, soft instrumental music was playing. The lights were low, and images of animals and stars floated across the light green walls and ceiling.

Oliver was already in his crib, his butt in the air. Selena had Sawyer on the changing table. "Does Finn need a change?" she asked him.

"Affirmative."

She held Sawyer out to him and they exchanged boys. As he held him, he swayed and told Sawyer about the airplanes he had been in. The small ones that took him into the wildest jungles and the huge planes that took him across the oceans.

He stroked the dark curls away from the tiny face as he studied the perfect little features. Sawyer's lids grew heavy and his head lay against Xavier's chest. He wanted to burn this image into his brain where it would never go away, no matter what happened or how old he got.

Gentle hands separated them. "Nice job. You got him to sleep." Selena kissed the boy on his head and turned to put him in the empty crib.

She stood there for a while, looking down on him. "They're outgrowing their cribs," she whispered, before turning to him. She jerked her head to the door and he followed her.

Going to the front of the landing, she paused at the

reading nook. "Do you want to go to the balcony? Do you think it will help your memories?"

His heart lurched. What if it did unlock forgotten moments? Was he ready for the truth? What if he hadn't loved her at all and that was the reason he couldn't remember?

Swallowing back the fear, he nodded, then stepped through the door behind her.

Chapter Eight

She sighed, pushed back the sheer white panel hanging over the glass door and opened it. She stood to the side and waited for him to join her. Without a word, he stepped onto the large balcony.

The front was wide-open, with a view over smaller houses right to the Gulf. The sides were surrounded by tall walls that went up to the roofline. Another small balcony was above them. "What's up there?"

"Oh, that's more for show than any real use. The attic is up there. We had talked about turning it into a huge family playroom with maybe a guest room, but it needs a lot to make it livable and it would need easier access. Right now, the only way up there is a pull-down ladder in the guest room. We decided converting the garage was easier. It had been an add-on and you wanted to tie it in better. It stuck out."

He nodded, then turned to the Gulf view. The waves rolled onto the beach, pelicans diving into the water. Way off on the horizon he could make out structures. "Do you spend a lot of time up here?"

"I have a coffeemaker in my room, so in the early

morning when the boys want to play and the weather is nice, I bring them out here. I go over my schedule and sip my first cup of coffee. It's my favorite time of the day."

Against one wall were two chairs with a small table between them. A colorful area rug made for a nice play area. He sat in the chair closest to the wall.

"What are the plans for the rest of the week?" He tilted his head back and let the sounds of the small-town wash over him.

"At midnight tonight, I have to go to the plaza. This is the first time we're lighting a town tree and I want to make sure all the lights work before the official ceremony. Sunday is church and choir practice. Monday you have PT and an appointment with the…"

She looked to the sky as if her calendar was floating there. "Eye doctor. Dad will have to take you. I have meetings that morning. Jazz and Elijah will have the boys."

"What?" He laughed. "Are you sure we can survive without you grilling the doc?"

"Oh, don't worry. My father will have a list of questions, and he'll record the session for me in case y'all forget key points."

"Of course. How could I have doubted you?"

"Tuesday—"

He held his hand up. "Three days in advance is more than enough for me." He tilted his head back. Taking deep breaths, he relaxed his body joint by joint. He allowed his thoughts to float, and he heard music weave its way around the clouds.

Without opening his eyes, he went deeper into the memory that wrapped itself around him. "We danced out here."

"We did." Her voice was low, far in the distance. She made a strangled noise and he turned to her. His hand was on top of hers without a thought. "Are you okay?"

She took a deep breath. "Yeah. Just stuck between a laugh and a hard sob. We danced to one song more than all the others. It was the last dance at our wedding."

"'Faithfully'?" He didn't understand why she would want to laugh, but she did say it was a nervous habit.

"Nope. This one is much more ironic." She pulled out her phone and played a song, holding it up for him to hear.

Head down, he concentrated. Then it hit him, and his gaze flew to hers. "Really?"

"Yes." She smiled, but the sadness in her eyes was heavy. "See what I mean? Cry or laugh?"

The soulful voice of Nat King Cole was joined by his daughter as they sang "Unforgettable." Selena joined them. There was no laughter in her new tears.

He stood and pulled her into his arms, swaying to the notes that floated around them. "Hush." He pressed his lips against her ear, his heart breaking as he tried to think of a way to stop her hurting. But he was the cause and he didn't know how to be the man she remembered or needed. "It's going to be all right."

He wanted to kiss her. To savor everything about her, but until he could remember, he didn't have that rights.

She nodded against his chest. Then "Unchained Melody" by the Righteous Brothers played. He held her tighter. The words ripped at his heart. How many times had she waited for him?

"I'm so sorry, baby."

She took a deep breath and pulled away. Reaching for her phone, she stopped the next song, Olivia Newton-John singing "I Honestly Love You." "Sorry about that.

That was my 'woe is me' playlist for when I need a good cry."

He hated the uselessness that numbed his limbs. "What happened, Selena? I mean in our marriage. Something wasn't right. From everything I've seen and heard from others, we had a perfect marriage. But…"

A gust of cold wind swirled around them. Selena pulled her sweater more tightly around herself, but she wouldn't look at him. Her gaze stayed on the horizon.

"Every couple has their problems," she said. "Did being here help you remember? Did the music?"

Hands deep in his pockets so he wouldn't reach for her, he studied the same horizon. The words to express his feelings escaped him. "Yes and no. It's like I was holding on to a ladder about to board the boat I needed to get back, but then the rope was cut, and I fell. I can see the boat, but it's getting farther away, and I can't swim fast enough. What happened between us? Was it my missions?"

Selena couldn't bring herself to look at him. There had been so much love between them in the beginning, and then she had pushed him away. "It was complicated."

He snorted. "Like a Facebook status?"

She glanced at the door. If the world was kind, someone would barge onto the balcony with an emergency and save her from this conversation.

She waited. No interruptions. One deep breath, then she turned back to the endless sky. "Your missions were part of the problems we were having. Or maybe they were your solution to what you were dealing with. I don't know. We fell in love really young. You remember our school dances?"

"I remember you were gorgeous." One side of his lips quirked up. "You still are. In a deeper, richer way."

A strange sound came from her throat. Running her hand along the weathered railing, she studied the horizon. "We were voted best couple. As soon as we got out of high school, we married. All you wanted was to leave Port Del Mar as far behind as you could. I wanted to make it my permanent home, the white picket fence, seven kids, a couple of dogs." She made herself look at him. "I thought once you got away from your father you would love my idea of family life. I was going to show you how perfect it could be and you would lose the desire to run."

He blinked at her. "Sorry, I didn't hear much more after seven kids." He had his hand over his heart as if to slow it down. "But I didn't buy into your dream?"

"No. You joined the army. I was really proud of you and thought it would help you get whatever it was out of your system. And then we would settle down here."

He looked over his shoulder, then back to her. "What happened to the seven kids?"

"Didn't happen. The first year we had a miscarriage." That seemed so long ago, but just like yesterday at the same time. She played with the tiny silver angel charm on the necklace he had given her.

Strong arms came around from behind her and he pulled her against his chest. "I'm so sorry. I didn't just leave you, did I?" The horror in his voice made her turn around to look him in the eye.

"No. You stayed with me and promised you'd never leave me again and we'd have other babies." She cupped his face. "We were only nineteen. I went with you when you were stationed in Germany. Each month I would fall

into a depression when I discovered I wasn't pregnant. I pulled away from you. I think you felt helpless for not being able to fix the problem, but we didn't know how to talk about it. I came home. After a few more years, you retired from the army. We bought this house and I thought you would finally stay."

"I didn't."

"No. Some friends of yours were doing private security and making good money. You joined them. And I started fertility treatments."

"But I was still leaving?" He scowled. "Why would I leave if we…"

"I came to the conclusion that I was lying to myself by thinking you would stop roaming the world and want to settle down in Port Del Mar. I couldn't make your heart want what I wanted. You were a hero out in the world, but with me? I think you felt like a failure."

He pressed his lips against the side of her head. She closed her eyes and absorbed the feeling of being in his arms. She had thought this was gone forever.

Xavier was here. But she couldn't change what he didn't feel or remember. In some ways, he was still just as far out of her reach.

His issues with his father and those stupid insecurities had been bigger than her love for him. She didn't see how now would be any different. If she gave him her heart again, they'd end up in the same place. Hurt. The only difference was the boys.

God, what do You want from me?

"Selena, I'm so sorry I can't… I don't know what to do. All I know is that I don't want to hurt you, but that seems to be all I'm capable of."

"You're a good man, Xavier De La Rosa. I don't know

where we are right now." She placed a firm hand on his chest. "You have one job and that's to follow your doctors' orders. We'll figure the rest out as we go."

She stepped back and looked into those magnificent gray-green eyes. The eyes that had been passed on to her sons. "I've learned to turn everything over to God." She laughed. "I'm better, anyway. We have the best Christmas gift." She reached up and cupped his face. "You're here. And those three little boys in there get to know their father. As you heal we'll find out how this new us will look on a daily basis." She shrugged. "God has this. No regrets. Okay?"

Xavier opened his mouth, but a door closed below them. Jazz, Belle, Elijah and their girls all stood in the front yard. The girls waved. Belle had the biggest smile on her face.

"See. I told y'all they'd be on the balcony." She waved. "The tamales are done and stored. Buelita said she was going to take a nap in her room. If y'all need anything, just call."

Selena leaned over the balcony. "Thanks for helping. It was fun." She watched as they all got in their cars and drove away. Xavier moved farther away from her.

After everything she'd just blurted out to him, she wasn't sure what to say. That had been too much at once.

She had way overshared. Closing her eyes, she said a quick prayer then turned, only to find him with his head down. He was rubbing the back of his neck.

"Xavier." She kept her voice low. "Is your head hurting?"

"A little." The reply was gruff.

"I gave you too much information."

"No. I'm fine. I just need to rest. There was a lot going

on today." He straightened his spine and rolled his shoulders, his face turned to the sky. "I'm going to my room."

She followed him in and down the stairs. "I'll be in the office working if you need anything."

At his door, he turned and gave her a reassuring smile, but the guilt was still heavy in his eyes. "Thank you."

"De nada." It was so much more than nothing, but today she didn't have many choices so why bother with drama. She waved him off, pretending all was right in her world, and quickly moved to her office. Sitting at the desk, she took some deep breaths. Seeing the guilt in his eyes when it wasn't his fault was the worst.

At one point he had been her everything and if anyone had told her he would stop loving her, she wouldn't have believed it. But his words on the day she thought they hadn't conceived would be forever burned into her brain.

Maybe it's all for the best.

He'd actually said the negative test result was for the best. When he'd left after those words, she'd known it was over and had called the lawyer before Xavier's plane had left the ground.

How could he not remember saying the words that had torn her heart out?

Stay in the moment. The past couldn't be changed. There was so much to do. For over a year her work for Christmas by the Sea had kept her focused and happy. It was a dream becoming a reality.

Studying her calendar, she organized the timeline in her head. But it was all a mess. She was losing control. She couldn't wrangle her thoughts from Xavier. What if he wanted more of the boys?

Closing her eyes, she stopped that downward spiral.

This was going to be the best Christmas and the boys had their father.

Sort of.

Pressing her hands together, she lowered her head and prayed, praising God for all the wonderful gifts He had brought to her door. This house would be full of Christmas joy and hope for the New Year.

Lifting her head, she scanned the wall and all the events—and realized she had forgotten to schedule one very important Christmas activity.

She hadn't set time aside to decorate the house and put up their personal Christmas tree.

Chapter Nine

Xavier sat straight up in bed. Despite the cool air, sweat trickled down his spine. He checked his phone—3:27. It was too early to be up.

He didn't remember having a bad dream. During his captivity and then after he'd been released from the local hospital, his sleep had been interrupted by constant night terrors.

Not even one had plagued him since he'd been in Port Del Mar. But this didn't feel like a night terror. Had something else woken him up?

Though uneasy, he slid back under his covers. A heavy thump on the ceiling brought him straight up in bed again. Had it been his imagination? When he heard another thunk, he knew it hadn't been.

What was that? Had someone broken into the house? Riff had taken a one-night gig and wasn't home.

It happened again, right over him. In the spare room above him. Someone was moving around upstairs. It was too heavy for the boys, unless they were moving furniture. He had watched too many of those videos on the internet the last week or two.

Swinging his legs from the bed, he slipped on his boots, waiting next to his bed.

He reached for his heavy-duty flashlight and went into the living room. He heard it again. Hyperaware, he took the stairs slowly.

At the top of the landing, he saw all the bedroom doors closed except for the spare. He checked on the boys. They were still sound asleep. Another noise came from above him.

Someone was in the attic. Pushing the guest bedroom door open, he swung the light around the room.

There were a few pieces of old furniture, but for the most part it was empty. The trapdoor to the attic was open and the ladder extended. At the base of the ladder was a green tub on its side. The lid was off and what looked to be Christmas decorations were inside. That's what he had heard.

Halfway up the ladder, he paused and listened. Whoever was crawling around in the attic was to his left. Easing up, he took one step at a time until he could see into the space. He heard muttering, followed by something being kicked.

Selena had her hands on her hips, glaring at a large tub.

"Selena. What's—"

She screamed and jumped back. Losing her balance, she fell into a stack of plastic containers behind her. "Xavier De La Rosa, you scared me half to death." She stood and checked on the boxes behind her.

Climbing into the attic, he joined her and set the stack back in place. "Sorry." He swung the flashlight around the area. The attic ran the length of the house and there wasn't an empty corner. "You scared me right out of a good night's sleep. I thought we were being invaded by giant river rats."

"Rats scurry. I don't scurry."

He brought the light around and aimed it at her worn teddy bear slippers and faded flannel pajamas. "I don't know. You're about the size of a big rat. In the jungle they were big enough to saddle. If I could have roped one, I'd have been home sooner."

Hands on hips, she went back to the long tub. "Not funny. But it might have been the rats that ate my tree."

Standing next to her, he looked down at the coffin-length box. Shredded fake pine needles made a nice bed for a Christmas tree skeleton. "That doesn't look good. Why are you throwing things around at three in the morning? Is it some sort of weird workout?"

"No. The boys should be asleep for a few more hours. It's about the only time I have to get the tree down and decorated. In all my planning for the town and getting ready for Christmas I forgot to put 'decorate the house' on my calendar. I was trying to squeeze it in."

"At three o'clock in the morning? Why are you being so stubborn about asking for help? I could have gotten these for you. You're doing too much. Let me help while I'm here." As soon as the words were out of his mouth, he knew he'd said the wrong thing. "Selena, I—"

"That's the problem. You're leaving. I can't allow my-self the luxury of your assistance. I'll be raising these boys alone. That's not a complaint. It's just the cold, hard truth and I need to get used to it. It's okay." She put the lid back on the long box. "My whole life, if I wanted some-thing, I had to do it myself. I want those boys down there to grow up with—" Her lips went into a tight, thin line.

"Selena—"

She held out her hand, not wanting him any closer. "It's okay. I'm stronger because of it. Everything in my past has prepared me to be their mother. All they will know from their childhood memories is the wonder of life and how joyful this time of the year is. When we celebrate love, giving and—" A hiccup cut off her words.

He set the flashlight down and pulled her into his arms.

With halfhearted effort, she pushed at him.

He didn't let go. "It's going to be okay."

"I'm not so sure. You hate Christmas. You always have and I'm tired of forcing others to—" Wiping her face, she stepped out of his arm. "I shouldn't have said that. I'm just tired. Your father didn't give you any reason to love this time of year."

He wanted to pull her back and tell her he didn't hate Christmas, but that would have been a lie.

The forest of boxes was neatly stacked and looked to be color coded. Each had a label and a picture. Outdoor, Tabletop, Mantel, Angels. She had it all neatly sorted.

"My therapist asked me about Christmas." He hated talking about this stuff, but he hated her tears even more. Tears he had put there.

If his talking would distract her, then he would.

"I thought y'all were working to retrieve memories." She put down the small box with gingerbread men dancing on the outside and stared at him, waiting for more.

He had her full attention, and the tears had stopped.

Great, now he had to talk. "Yeah. Well, she thinks part of the memory blockage has to do with emotions I've submerged. Submerged emotion can lead to memory and word blockage." He curled his lip.

She crossed her arms and raised an eyebrow. "That doesn't sound pleasant."

With a grin he shrugged. Mission accomplished. Not a tear in sight.

"Her words, not mine. Anyway. I mentioned how much I hate Christmas, even though I can't really remember it. She told me to write down triggers. When I get upset and want to shut down or go another direction, I'm supposed to journal what brought on the 'feelings.'" He did air quotes with his hands.

"Have you done that? I know that Christmas can be a stressful time for some people. Especially if—" Biting her lip, she gave him an uncertain glance.

"There's a history of abuse?" He couldn't look at her. His throat all of a sudden felt raspy, dry. Where was a glass of water when he needed one?

"I'm sorry. I was always trying to change your attitude about Christmas. I didn't truly understand your defiance."

"You had a lousy childhood, too. But instead of hating it, you ran around trying to make Christmas the best thing ever for everyone."

"People react differently. I overcompensate. You avoid. Plus, my father never hurt me or made me feel small. He just loved music and traveling more than—" She shook her head. "Did she give you any advice what to do with the journals and your feelings?"

"Triggers are usually bad things. She suggested that I create new positive events and memories to replace them." He crossed his arms over his chest and looked around the attic. "But what I really want to know is why you're kicking the Christmas boxes you love."

Dropping to her knees, she pushed the lid back and scooped up a handful of plastic pine needles. They slipped through her fingers. "I was going to sneak the tree down while the boys were sleeping, but something got into the box and now the tree's ruined."

He shrugged. "We'll go buy a new one. Your dad and I can go. We can even take the boys."

She shook her head. "This tree was supposed to last another five years. I don't have a new tree in the budget. And buying a tree right before Christmas is not good. Do you know the markup? The best time to get a tree is after Christmas, when they go on sale."

Xavier chuckled. "Ms. Christmas Surprise is being all practical."

"With my budget, yes." She stood. "I can figure something else out."

"Since we're up here and wide-awake, which boxes do you want to take down? Where are your nativity scenes? Those are your favorites and the first thing you always pulled out."

Wide-eyed, they stared at each other. "That's right. You remembered."

He grinned. "I remembered."

With a smile, she nodded to a stack of purple tubs. "They're in those two boxes. It's a good place to start. Thank you." Head tilted, she bit her lip. "How does that happen? You remember the most random things, but not…" She shrugged. "The big stuff. I would think it would be the other way around."

Moving to the stack she indicated, he lifted the lid to the top box and tried to come up with a way to explain. On the top in silver tissue paper lay a snow globe with the Holy Family depicted in fine details.

He picked it up and turned it upside down and swirled the white flakes. "It's kind of like I'm stuck in a snow globe. I know you're there, but I can't get to you. I'll reach out and grab something that's floating by and pull it in. It's connected to the place I'm trying to get to. I'm thinking of you and you mention decorating for Christmas. Wham, I find the nativity scenes you collected." He watched as the snow settled over the manger inside the globe. "I gave you this one. Brought it back from one of my trips. Italy?"

"Yes." She pushed the box with the ruined tree out of the way. Silently, she grabbed a purple box and moved to the attic ladder.

"Let me take that." He caught up with her.

"No. I've got it. I'm used to doing this by myself every year anyway."

And just like that the easy camaraderie was gone. She maneuvered down the ladder with the box like a pro. After making sure she was safe, he restacked all her Christmas boxes at the opening. When she came back, he stopped her. "I thought this might be faster instead of going up and down one tub at a time."

Going halfway down the ladder, he handed her another purple box.

"I'm not sure you should be on a ladder. What if you lose your balance? I can do this."

"But you don't have to and I'm not going up and down." He bounced. "It's solid and I'm just handing you boxes so neither of us has to climb this thing." Twisting, he took the box off the edge of the platform and passed it to her.

Taking the box, she nodded, but didn't say anything else. Once the purple ones were down, he moved to the red ones, marked Outdoors. The next to go were the silver ones marked Other.

"Don't bother with the green boxes. Those are the ornaments for the tree."

"You'll have a tree." There were a lot of things he didn't get right, and he couldn't fix, but he could do this for her.

"Xavier, don't worry about it. I have plenty of decorations."

He didn't bother disagreeing with her as he made plans. He needed to make a few calls and talk to her father. He left the green boxes in the attic and came down and lifted the ladder back into the ceiling. He could imagine what would happen if the little guys discovered it down. They'd see it as a personal invitation to explore.

He picked up a purple box and followed her down the stairs. They moved quietly so as not to disturb anyone else in the house. It was like they were the only two people in the world. Once all the boxes were in the living room, he looked around. "What's next?"

"You should probably go back to bed and get a couple of hours of sleep."

"When do you sleep?"

"I'm not the one recovering from head trauma." Lifting the pieces out of the tub, she unwrapped each one before setting it on the coffee table.

"No, but you are a mother of three toddlers and from what I can see you have a whole town you're taking care of. When do you get to rest?"

Her shoulders rose and fell with a heavy sigh. "I love all the gifts God has given me and I want to...make sure I don't take those gifts for granted. I get all the rest I need. Right now, I want to set up my nativities."

His hand closed over her fingers as she cradled a baby Jesus. "Everyone loves you so much, Selena. You don't have to work so hard to earn it. You know you already have it, right?"

Her throat closed up at the thought of all those people loving her.

Moving away from him, she gently placed the wood carved figurines on the mantel. "That's not why I do this. I had no one growing up. You might not remember, but you did give me a family and this town. A place that took me in and accepted me, gave me a real home. A home I can give my sons. I want to give back to all of them. Belle, Elijah and Damian had the same Christmas experiences as you. They have been a great gift to me. I want to give back to them."

He chuckled and crossed his arms as he leaned on the mantel. "You had to be in bad shape if you're thanking me for giving you the De La Rosa family. What I remember would be better off forgotten."

Fire in her eyes, she turned to him. "Don't do that. Your father and aunt had issues and should have been reported to the authorities. After the death of your mother, you stepped in and pretty much raised your siblings and cousins. You made them into adults that are hardworking and loyal. I love them, and they have been there for me in my dark—" She bit her lip and lowered her head.

Great. Now he'd upset her. In a few steps, he had her in his arms. "I'm sorry."

"I won't let you talk bad about them. They do the same thing. I hate it when they put themselves down. They're the best."

"I know. I was just joking. The De La Rosas don't take compliments well. I thank God they were there for you when I wasn't."

"Mama?" came from the stairs above.

She groaned. "There goes my Secret Santa mission. They must have heard us."

"Let me go up and see if I can get them back to sleep. They should be down for a couple more hours, right?"

"Mama?" A thump followed this time.

"Sawyer just made his escape. Do you mind? If they give you problems, just bring them down and they can play awhile before breakfast."

He was halfway up the stairs when he had an idea. "Selena, what time does your meeting wrap up today?"

"Eleven, but sometimes they go a little over. Why? Is there a problem?"

"Nope. So, you can be home a little before noon?"

She narrowed her eyes. "Yes. But I have an additional choir practice and the ladies at—" She stopped. "Why?"

"I just had a great idea for lunch with the boys and wanted to make sure you could join us."

"Daddy." Sawyer appeared at the safety gate at the top of the stairs with his favorite blanket and toy. He threw the floppy horse over the gate and watched it bounce.

Xavier took the steps two at a time and scooped up the toy. "Hey, little man." His bottom was saggy, in a very suspicious way. "Seems we know where we need to start. Clean diaper for you while I tell you about the wonders of indoor plumbing."

The little boy giggled. Xavier took a moment to absorb the wonder of holding his child. The tiny fingers twined in his hair as they made their way to the bedroom the boys shared.

The other two were awake and standing in their cribs. "Yeah, I see y'all acting all innocent, like you're the rule followers. I'm not buying it."

He laid Sawyer on the changing table. "They told you

to come out and get us, didn't they? Don't let them set you up like that." Sawyer reached up and grabbed his nose. Xavier laughed.

Finishing him up and setting him on the floor, he went to Finn. "Come on, your turn. So, I have this idea to help your mom with Christmas." The boy babbled something back to him.

"I know, right?" They carried on the conversation until he was dry and changed.

With the second child on the ground, Xavier was feeling accomplished. This wasn't so hard. He went to get Oliver.

The youngest triplet was sitting in the far corner of his crib. He pulled the cover over his head when Xavier approached. "Hey, I totally get it. You don't know me. It's cool that you hold back, but right now I'm in charge of changing you and making sure you go back to sleep so your mother can get some work done. Maybe even sleep. Let's do this." He pulled at the blanket.

Oliver buried himself deeper under the blanket and screamed. His brothers stopped what they were doing and looked at them like Xavier had done something wrong.

"What? I'm just trying to change him like I did you. Tell him it's okay." He turned back to Oliver and tried to pick him up. The boy stiffened his body and arched his back.

Not sure what to do, Xavier sat him back on his bed. "Shh. I'm not going to hurt you." He held his hands up and palms out, but that didn't seem to help.

The door opened and Riff came in, still wearing his stage clothes. "What's all the ruckus about?"

The two on the floor started explaining. That's what

Xavier assumed, anyway. He didn't understand a word they said.

"How was the gig?"

Riff shrugged. "It was good. But I thought I'd miss it more. It was nice to know I'd be home instead of on the road when it was done. Need help?"

"I changed these two with no problems. Oliver isn't having any of it."

"He's not much of a morning person and he hates having his diaper changed. He doesn't do well with any type of change, as I'm sure you noticed. He is totally his mother's child. She hated change of any kind."

"But she spent most of her childhood traveling with you."

"Yep and was just about the sourest kid you'd ever meet. I didn't really get it until she moved in with Buelita. Poor kid. I just thought she was grumpy by nature. I was kind of clueless as a father."

Riff handed a plush puppy to Oliver and kissed him on the forehead, saying something too low for Xavier to hear. Then he started singing to him and picked him up, rocking him against his shoulder before laying him down on the changing table.

"Why didn't you let her move in with Buelita sooner?"

"She never asked. I would have let her if I understood the problem. I think she also thought she was being loyal by staying with me. With her mom leaving us when she was just a tyke, she didn't want to make me sad. That's what the counselor told me, anyway. Sounds about right. My dream was being on the road, playing my music across the country. I would have thought it was a dream come true as a kid."

He sang to Oliver a little bit more before making a

move to change him. "With this one you have to move slow, let him adjust. He'll get used to you, and when he does his trust is deep." Riff slipped off the used diaper and slipped on the clean one in a smooth move. "You're a traveler like I was. Are you going to be around long enough for him to trust you?"

Xavier sat on the floor, stacking blocks with Finn as Sawyer knocked them down. "Did you ask me that when I married Selena?"

"Nope. I wasn't a very astute father. Unfortunately for Selena, it took some aging before I gained any wisdom. You and I got along, and I thought you'd be great for Selena. You'd show her the world. I didn't understand that she didn't want to see the world. That was my dream." He started singing a haunting ballad as he joined them on the floor. Oliver leaned on his chest, sucking his thumb. Finn yawned.

"A home in this small town was her dream. And a family." Xavier was starting to wonder why Selena had married him. It seemed he was traveling to parts unknown more than he was home. Finn crawled into his lap and rested against him.

"She has her dream. How do I play a part in her life now? I still have work to do. People need me." Did she need him? He looked at Oliver asleep on his grandfather's lap.

"I don't give advice any longer. We each have to go deep into our own hearts and be true to what we find there, what God planted there. I have no way of knowing what is in your heart. All I know now is that I don't know half of what I thought I knew." Riff gently got up and laid Oliver back into his bed. "I love the people in my life and try to give back to those I took so much from."

"Are you happy here?" Xavier put Finn in his bed, then picked up the most restless of the triplets and rocked him.

Riff took Sawyer from him and laid him in his bed, pulling the light blanket over his head. Patting the boy's back, he smiled. "I'm where I need to be. I'm too old to be spending my life on a bus." He paused. "These boys might have the hearts of traveling warriors or deep roots in their hometown, but either way they will know they have a safe place where they're loved, where they belong."

He looked at Xavier. "That's all any of us really want. My Selena is giving that to her boys." He made his way to the door.

In the hallway, he sighed. "That should give us another couple of hours. Why don't you get some rest before we start the day? You have PT and an eye appointment today, right?"

"Yeah. I have a favor to ask you. I want to make some calls and maybe take a day trip with Selena and the boys. If I can get the details worked out, will you join us and surprise Selena with making a Christmas memory as a family? We'd need to have the boys ready to go as soon as she gets home. I told her I have a special lunch planned."

"That girl of mine lives to make Christmas memories. Count me in." He went to his room.

Xavier couldn't resist looking in on the boys one more time. They were so sweet and innocent in the cribs they were outgrowing. He smiled. Sawyer wiggled in his sleep and turned over. Walking to Oliver's bed, he gently put his hand on his youngest son's back. "You might be the smartest of the group. I'd love to promise you that I'd be the father you need, but I'm not sure I know how to be a father. But that's okay, because you have one awesome mother. She deserves the best of everything."

Not some broken-down half of a man that couldn't even remember her. But he could give her a Christmas tree to remember.

Chapter Ten

The meeting had been so long today, and all Selena seemed to care about was the lunch Xavier had planned. He'd never been the plan-a-date kind of man.

Mail in hand, she stopped at the doorway of her house where Xavier stood. She frowned. "Why are the boys bundled up to go outside? I thought we were having lunch."

Xavier crossed his arms and grinned at her. "Because they are going outside. I never said where we were having lunch."

Riff walked in the room and picked up Sawyer. Swinging the giggly boy over his shoulder, he kissed his daughter on the cheek. "So…you excited? This will be so much fun. Sounds like something you always wanted to do."

"Maybe if someone told me what was going on, I could be excited instead of confused."

"Woad tip." Finn clapped, then hugged Oliver around the neck. Cupping his face, he told his brother a secret.

"Kismas twee," Sawyer yelled.

"It was supposed to be a surprise." Xavier looked at

his father-in-law, then back to Selena. "Your father, the boys and I have planned a special trip for you."

"Trip?" She dropped the mail on the foyer table and her hands went to her hips. "I have choir practice and I'm helping at the shelter with sorting—"

"Twee. Twee. Oh Kismas twee." All three boys started singing.

"I called everyone that was expecting you and explained the situation. They have all given you permission to play hooky for the rest of the day. You'll be all ready for the big day tomorrow. The parade is all set, right? I know you'd want to be in town for that."

"Xavier De La Rosa, I told you I will figure something out. I'm not buying a new tree this time of year."

Her dad picked up Oliver with his free arm and placed him on his hip. "Come on, babe. This is not the time to be practical. Your husband planned a special trip for us. Let's get in the car and find out what adventure awaits."

She glared at her father's back. That was the problem. She didn't trust Xavier in this role of husband. He'd recover his memories and she'd be left with a broken heart again. And three little boys that now had a face for their father wouldn't understand his leaving.

The boys all cheered and clapped and yelled. This wasn't fair. If she said no, she'd be the bad guy.

Xavier got her long red coat out of the front closet and was holding it out for her to slip her arms into. "The temperature dropped today, and it's supposed to get colder." He leaned in close and his peppermint scent softened her as he whispered against her ear. "I'm trying to create new memories here. New triggers. Are you gonna help a lost Scrooge out?"

"That is not how you use the word *triggers*. Plus, that's

not fair." She buttoned her coat. "Are we going to a place that sells trees locally?"

Xavier picked up Finn, tickling the boy. "What's the fun of you knowing where we're going if it's supposed to be a surprise?" Tossing Finn over his shoulder, he headed to the door. "Come on, troops, we got a mission to accomplish and time is running out."

Selena took Oliver from her father. "Do we have their bags, sippy cups and snacks if they get hungry? What about extra clothes? With toddlers you have to be prepared for anything." She looked around. "We can't just leave with three babies." She looked at her dad.

Xavier opened the back door of her Suburban. Stretching over, he buckled in Sawyer. "Your dad packed everything and we're ready to go. Do you want to sit with the boys or do you want to ride shotgun?" He turned and accepted Finn from her father. It took him a little bit longer, but he got both boys secured in the far backseat.

She looked at her father. "You know what's going on?" She crossed her arms. "And we have everything the boys need?"

Her father took Oliver from her and got him settled in. Then he turned to her. "Do I need to buckle you in, too?" He hugged her. "Anyone ever tell you you've got to learn to roll with it? Xavier has planned a road trip for the family. You can be grumpy and all practical or you can embrace the day and enjoy whatever may come. Life is about creating memories, babe, and today we are creating a memory. Get that phone of yours ready to take the pictures of a lifetime."

"Okay. I'll ride back here with Oliver. Xavier, you should be in the front. Less car sickness there."

Xavier held the door and motioned her to get in. "New

memories for a new and improved life." He winked at her. Soon they were all settled in and heading out of town, crossing the bridge to the mainland.

"What are we doing? If I'm going to have to spend a lot of money on a new tree, at least do it locally. Going to some big box store in the city will not help our economy."

From the driver's seat, her dad made eye contact with her in the rearview mirror. "Looks like Grumpy Gus is back."

"Gumpy Gus," Finn repeated.

Xavier grinned at her. "Are we only allowed to support Port Del Mar businesses? How about supporting another small town's mom-and-pop business?" There was pure happiness on his face. The boys were excited.

She took a deep breath and pushed out the bad energy she had been holding on to.

Twisted against his seat belt, her husband looked at her. There was a twinkle in his eyes she hadn't seen in over five years. "Have you always been this set against fun and surprises, or am I just forgetting this about you?"

Rolling her eyes, Selena crossed her arms. "I can be spontaneous if given enough chance to plan things and make sure everything is—" She pulled up short when Xavier and Riff both fell into laughter.

The boys joined in, even though they had no clue why their father and grandfather were laughing.

How could she not smile? Relaxing, she sat back and enjoyed the sound of happiness that filled her car.

"This ain't nothing new." Her father looked at Xavier. "From the time she could talk and walk, she wanted to plan. Drove me crazy. You were always good for her, making her loosen up."

"I thought this would be a fun surprise," Xavier told

her. "Your dad made sure the boys are ready for an all-day trip. If you want me to, I'll tell you exactly what you're going to—"

"All day?" She scowled at him, her commitment to going with the flow already out the window. "Where are we going?"

"We're going to the Hill Country." The grin on his face got bigger. "I found a Christmas tree farm. They even have a snow machine, hot chocolate and Santa's favorite longhorn. The pictures on the website look great. I noticed all the photos you have of the boys. I thought you'd love the snow and trees. There's even a red wagon they can ride in while we go through the forest to pick a tree."

She stared at him as if he was speaking a different language. "Santa's longhorn?"

"Yep. His name is Rudy. The reindeers don't like coming this far south. Plus," he added as he winked at her, "I've never had a real Christmas tree. I'll get to chop it down and everything." He pointed to the boys dressed in red and green plaid with little red suspenders. "They're gonna pick out a tree just for their mom."

"Twee. Kismas twee."

"Mama twee."

All three boys talked over each other.

That did it. Her insides went soft and gooey as she looked at her sons.

"How far away is this Christmas tree farm?"

"It's about two and a half hours. But we have a couple stops on the way to make sure the boys can get out. It's all planned out. You're just not the one who planned it." He turned to face the road. "Lunch is at a roadside café with a playground."

She sat back. "Sounds like you thought of everything."

Pulling out her phone, she took a selfie of her and the boys. Stage one of their Christmas tree adventure.

A little over three hours after they left Port Del Mar, they turned down a long country road. Xavier looked back at his family. The boys had fallen asleep soon after they had left cafe. When she was first forced to sit still, Selena had dozed off, but she stared out the window now.

They passed under a wrought-iron gate that said Christmas Ranch. Along both sides of the dirt road was a wood fence decorated with greenery and red ribbon.

Longhorn cattle and other exotic animals grazed in the pastures. Selena woke up the boys. "Look, zebras."

Faces pressed to the windows, they made a bunch of excited noises. As they drove farther into the ranch, they saw barns and elaborate Christmas light displays.

Selena stared out the window. "They have lights everywhere. I wasn't expecting that."

"Lights were always her favorite part of Christmas," Riff said, as he turned off the main road. An arrow pointed the way to a red-and-white-striped sign welcoming them to the North Pole of Texas.

"Riff did a lot of shows during the Christmas season." She had the same wide-eyed wonder as the boys. "We never had a tree, but he would drive me around whatever city they were playing to see the Christmas lights."

"I didn't know you wanted a tree," her father grumbled. "We could have gotten a small one."

"We were on a bus. I just assumed Santa only went to houses. And why have a tree if there were no gifts?"

"Oh, baby. I didn't know… I can't… I'm sorry."

"It's okay. I saw more Christmas lights than any other kid in the world."

Everyone was getting sad and it was killing Xavier's new Christmas spirit. He needed to stop the spiral. "Are we ready to get the best Christmas tree ever?"

"Twee. Twee. Twee." Finn led the chant.

"We have a decision to make." He twisted around and winked at Selena. "Do we start with the Charlie Brown tree or go with the Paul Bunyan tree? What will fit your house?"

"My artificial tree was eight feet." She twisted her lips to the side as if she wanted to say more.

"Do you want to go taller?" He raised his brows.

Her gaze darted to her father, then back to him. "How tall do you think we could go?"

"With your ceilings? We could easily go ten feet. The Suburban can handle it. Let's do it!"

She shook her head. "No. That has to cost a fortune."

Riff joined his cause. "It's Xavier's first tree and he's home. We didn't think we'd ever have him with us again. I say we go for it. I'll help. I owe you for all the trees I never gave you."

"Oh, look. Planted Christmas trees. Maybe we can plant a Christmas tree in the city plaza. Each year we could decorate it as it grows."

"Hang on, girl," Riff told her. "One tree at a time. Today is all about you and the boys."

There were trees of all different sizes covered in snow. Something that looked like snow, anyway. A red-and-white-striped pole marked the offices. White lights were strung across the top, running to the trees nearby and completely surrounding a building that looked like a fairy-tale gingerbread house.

There was a lot full of cars, but not many people visible. Behind the gingerbread house was a playground and a cute little shed that had "Hot Chocolate" and "Apple Cider" hand painted across the top. More of the fake snow was piled along the edges of the fence.

The door to the office opened with a jingle. An older woman with her silver hair in a long braid that wrapped around her head greeted them with a big smile.

As they pulled the excited boys from the Suburban, Xavier was thankful they had a man-on-man defense.

"Welcome to the Christmas tree ranch." The storybook granny slipped her hands into the pockets of her red apron and pulled out an old-fashioned pocket watch. "You must be the De La Rosa family."

He grinned. "That we are."

"I'm Jill. My, my, my, what do we have here? I heard about you. This must be Oliver, Finn and Sawyer. Santa has said some very good things about you." She clapped her hands at the boys' wide-eyed expressions. "He told us to be ready for you to come and pick out a special Christmas tree for your mama. Is that you?"

They each bounced and clapped. "Kismas twee."

"Mama's new Kismas twee." Finn nodded with all the seriousness of an old man.

"Perfect. We have one just for her and you'll get to find it in Candy Cane Lane, right past Reindeer Drive. If you want to go play and get something to drink, I'll give your daddy all the information he needs."

Daddy. Xavier wasn't expecting that hit to his chest. It was the first time anyone had seen them as a normal family. At home everyone knew his story, but here he was just their daddy taking care of the details. For a moment, he wasn't sure he knew how to breathe.

A warm hand came to rest on top of his. "Xavier?" Concern laced Selena's soft voice.

He smiled at her and put Finn down. She took the toddler's hand before he could run off. "Are you okay?" Her voice was low.

"Yes. Just logging new triggers." He leaned closer to her. Wanting to kiss her. *Idiot.*

He quickly turned to Jill before he did something stupid.

She explained the map to him. Then she pulled out the biggest red wagon he had ever seen, complete with all-terrain wheels. With a smile, she sent him off to his family.

When he turned to the playground, he paused as he watched the triplets climbing and falling without fear. His family. Selena cupped her hot chocolate between her gloved hands as she laughed at the boys' antics. She took his breath away. More than just beautiful, she took care of her family and the whole town. Giving more than she took.

He knew in that moment that Selena had been his light and strength. All doubt about how he had felt for her was gone. His heart had always belonged to her, but he had left her when she had needed him the most.

She looked up and smiled at him. He had the power to put out that light. He'd done it before. Clearing his throat, he called out to the boys.

"Okay, men, follow me. We're going to the north pasture, the land of—" He looked at the map, then pointed. "Wild reindeer, until we find Candy Cane Lane. That's where we'll find our tree."

The boys cheered, repeating his words. "Waindea. Waindea. Canny Can. Canny Can."

With the large red wagon in hand, he offered to pull the boys, but they were too excited to sit still.

Riff laughed as he followed them, scooping up Sawyer before he took off too far from his brothers.

Selena shook her head. "Boys, where you going?" She chuckled. "Do you know where Candy Cane Lane is?"

Her father looked over his shoulder and pointed to the colorful signs that marked the way. Every few rows there was a candy-cane-striped pole with arrows showing the direction for the different pastures. Elf Avenue. Holly Street. North Star Road. Noel Lane.

Going to the west trail, the offices and fake snow gave way to Hill Country gorgeousness. The little valley sat snug in the middle of greenery, surrounded by rolling hills.

Selena grabbed Xavier's free hand. "It's so beautiful, I could live here. Thank you."

"Thank you, for letting me do this for the boys and... and you." So many emotions swam in his chest that he couldn't find any more words. His chest vibrated with a frustrated growl.

"Xavier?" Selena searched his eyes. "Are you okay? Do we need to go back?"

Shaking his head, he broke eye contact and stared at the boys. Finn and Oliver held hands as they danced and jumped around their grandfather. Sitting on Riff's shoulders, Sawyer pointed to the signs, laughing and yelling at his brothers.

They didn't know they had a broken father.

Another family passed by and everyone waved a friendly greeting.

Selena pressed against his side. "They're having a great time. Even Dad. I never even imagined this kind of holiday tradition." She pulled out her phone and took a few pictures of her sons and father walking through the Christmas wonderland.

Riff slid Sawyer to the ground but held his hand before letting him go with a warning.

He took a deep breath. "My guess is the wagon is for the trip home when they're too exhausted to walk anymore."

Sawyer ran ahead, then back. Zigzagging, he fell once, but was up and running again before anyone could respond. Oliver headed to his mom.

"Tethers might be a good idea for those two," Xavier said as he surveyed the area. "It would be easy to lose them."

"They usually don't go too far from me. This enchanted forest has them overly excited."

"Was this a bad idea?"

"Oh, no. This is amazing. Before, you would have gone out, bought me another fake tree, set it up and proclaimed to have the problem solved. Didn't matter if I wanted it or not." She waved her hand around her. "To plan this for all of us to have a Christmas experience together? Seriously, thank you."

His throat felt itchy. Making sure to relax and enjoy the moment, he smiled at her. "A side benefit of forgetting who I am. We can make a new and improved me as we go along."

"The old you wasn't that bad. He had his moments."

Once they got to the correct pasture for their tree, the triplets were turned loose to pick one. The adults did more laughing as they darted from one perfect tree to another.

After about the tenth tree, Xavier was ready to call

it. He carried the ax over his shoulder and stood behind Selena.

"This looks like a winner to me. What do you think, Mom?" The boys surrounded him as they all looked at her and waited.

"They're all so beautiful." She looked at him.

Oh, no. She had tears in her eyes. He had called her "mom" He frowned and went back to staring at the tree. He hadn't meant to say it, it just happened. "Selena—"

"But this one here…" She wiped at her face, then a soft laugh followed. Now she was laughing. "This is the one that has been waiting for us."

The boys bounced with excitement, cheering. "Good job, guys. Let's take her home." There were a few piles of fake snow one row over. While Xavier swung the axe, Riff took the boys to play in it a safe distance away.

"Are you sure you can or should do this?" she asked Xavier when he was about halfway through the tree trunk.

He paused long enough to give her a look. She held her hands up. "Go for it."

A few steps back and she was with her dad and the boys. "You know, one of these days we'll have to take the boys to see real snow."

Her dad scoffed, then slipped forward and picked up Sawyer. Swinging the little boy over his shoulder upside down, he blew against the exposed round tummy.

"Snow is overrated," he said. "I hated the gigs where we had to drive through it. Give me the fake stuff any-day."

"Tree is down!" Xavier pulled a rope from his pocket. "I can pull it back to the car."

Her father brought the red wagon around with Sawyer sitting inside. Finn climbed in.

"Oh, I want to get a picture of all my men with the tree and wagon." Selena picked Oliver up and tried to hand him over to Xavier. "Here, hold him."

Oliver shook his head and clung to his mom. He turned his face away from Xavier.

"Come on, little man. Let me hold you so your mom can take a picture." Xavier didn't know many adults with the kind of stubborn chin he saw on Oliver. He had no choice but to concede defeat. "It's okay. Don't force him. Here, I'll take the Finn-man." With the ax leaning against his leg, he held his son on the opposite hip. "What about you? Let me take a few of you and the boys with your father."

"Oh, no." She turned her back to them and lifted the camera high. "Smile, everyone. Merry Christmas!" She took a few selfies. She and the boys made funny faces. Then she put the phone away. "Okay. Let's get this tree back to the house."

Riff offered to help, but Xavier needed something to focus on that was not his wife and sons. His family. It was dangerous to get too comfortable.

Somewhere in the back of his mind, he knew he had a mission to complete and until that was done he couldn't afford to settle.

Chapter Eleven

The tree was secured on the top of the Suburban and the boys, including Riff, were sound asleep. Xavier, though, was wide-awake, watching Selena as she drove. It had been such a perfect day and he had seen a smile on her face he hadn't seen.

Selena pulled up to the house but didn't put the SUV in Park. "Xavier, there's a man on our porch."

Strangers had a way of putting him on alert. He swallowed past the sudden dryness in his throat. Today had been so perfect...until now.

"It's going to be okay." He had an uneasy feeling that he should know the man. "So, you don't know him?"

She shook her head, then woke her dad.

Blinking his eyes, her father leaned forward.

"Do you recognize that man?" Selena looked back at Xavier. "Sometimes his old road buddies show up needing a place to crash."

"Sorry, baby. Never seen him before. He sees us staring at him, though. What should we do?"

Xavier reached for the door handle. "I'll speak with

him. Y'all take the boys to the ranch or somewhere safe. I'll call when all is clear."

"I'm not leaving you here alone." Even though her voice was low, he could hear the outrage.

"How will you help? And I doubt he's here to cause problems. He's sitting out in the open. All of the neighbors could identify him."

"Okay. That makes sense. But what if you need help? You know, with your sight or your voice or balance or something." She put the car in Park but didn't shut off the engine. "Dad, take the boys to visit Belle and the girls at the ranch. I'll call to let you know when to come home." Without another word, not even giving him a chance to argue, she was out of the car. Her father slipped into the driver's seat.

"Doesn't appear she's waiting for you," Riff said to Xavier as he grinned at him.

Xavier glared at him. "You think it's funny that you raised a stubborn daughter?"

"Hey, it got her through some really rough times. Go get her."

Ouch. He was the reason she needed to be so tough. No wonder she didn't trust him to stay.

A few strides and he caught up with her. He tried to put himself between her and the stranger. "Selena. Please stay behind me." He adjusted his hat and made sure he looked as if he didn't have a care in the world.

The man stood when they hit the steps. He had dark wavy hair and a big smile that showed off white teeth against his tan skin. He looked friendly and about the most nonthreatening male Xavier had seen since coming back to Port Del Mar. He wasn't buying it.

The man approached Xavier with his hand out, the

other reaching to clasp his shoulder. "Xavier. It's true! You're alive. Man, when the rumors started we didn't know what to believe. This is amazing." The man came in for a hug. Xavier stiffened.

"Excuse me. Who are you?" Now Selena was attempting to put herself between him and the stranger.

"Selena." Xavier tried to warn her to back off, but he wasn't sure how without making a scene.

The man laughed. "Sorry, ma'am. I'm Captain Roberto Diaz. But everyone calls me Beto. You must be Mrs. De La Rosa. It's a pleasure to meet you."

The man seemed open and sincere, but Xavier knew that was how the best traps worked.

A sweat broke out down his spine. Could he trust this man? Was it safe to let him know he had memory gaps? When it came to work, he had no memories. Just because this stranger threw a *captain* in front of his name didn't mean anything.

"How did you find me?" he asked. He needed a way to get info without giving any up.

Beto stepped back a little and narrowed his eyes. "When we got word you had survived, we were stunned. Heard there was a mistaken ID and head trauma. You still haven't recovered your memories? Since you were home, I figured healing was in progress."

Selena scanned the neighborhood. "Should we go in and sit down?" she asked Xavier.

Good question. He wasn't sure he wanted this man in his home. He shot a startled glance at Selena. That was the first time he had thought of this house as his home. When had it become his?

He gritted his back teeth. Now wasn't the time to analyze the words his brain was throwing around. "Why don't we talk here." He indicated the rockers on the front porch.

"I could bring tea or coffee." She was looking at him as she spoke. "I also need to check to see if Buelita is back from her friend's."

"Good idea. I could use tea. Thank you." He glanced at their guest. "Tea? Coffee?"

More subdued now, but still pleasant, their visitor nodded. "Coffee sounds good, thank you."

Once she was gone, Xavier sat on the edge of the porch swing and waved him to the rocking chair.

Beto sat, then leaned forward. "You don't know who I am, do you? How bad are the memory gaps?"

Xavier crossed his legs, then uncrossed them. He forced his rigid posture to relax into the corner of the swing. If he wanted to get anything useful from this guy, he needed to think clearly. That was part of the problem. Did he really want information he might have to act on?

He had no way of knowing if he trusted this man. He had been on dangerous jobs; what if the captain wasn't here to help? He leaned back and laced his fingers over his lap. Eyes narrowed, he studied Diaz.

The captain rested his elbows on his knees. "Okay, so I get it. You're having trust issues at the moment. Totally understandable. I'm going to pull my ID out." He lifted his hands palms out. "And some other information you might find helpful."

Pulling them from the inside of his jacket, he laid a photo ID and other papers on the table next to his chair. "You're part of an organization that focuses on undercover work to rescue and protect children from life-threatening situations. We've busted some pretty big human trafficking operations."

Xavier looked through the information.

"We do other off-the-record jobs, too. In Colombia you were on a more personal mission. A friend of a friend needed help pulling a child out of a high-risk environment. You were scheduled to meet up with Trent the next day, but we heard about the ambush. We were told you and the boy were dead. Trent stayed and did some follow-up, but we had no indications that the report was false, so we left the country. We weren't supposed to be there. Man, I don't know what to say other than sorry. If we'd had any indication you were the man they were calling Pedro Sandoval, we would have gone in. We would never have left you."

He looked at Beto. "How long have we been doing this?"

"Trent and I started the group ten years ago. You've been with us for about the last six years." Beto's dark eyes scanned Xavier's face. "How extensive is the memory loss?"

Xavier looked down at the documents. Everything seemed legit. He hoped he wasn't making a mistake in trusting this stranger. "I remember some of the early years in the army." He tilted his head back and let the memories he had flutter around until they settled in some sort of order. "Kuwait. I met you there. Then I remember being in Singapore, but that wouldn't have been with the army."

"That was your first trip with us, Cazador Company."

"Hunter?"

"Yeah. We're a high-end security company, but we also run a nonprofit that hunts human traffickers. You worked on that end."

Tray in hand, Selena came back to the porch. She set

it on the table between the rockers and handed out the cups. Xavier held the warm mug in both hands and studied the steam swirling and fading, like the memories he wanted most.

Something was slamming against his brain, something important.

She sat on the opposite end of the swing about a foot from him. Too far.

"Do you want me to go?"

"No. No more secrets."

He reached for Selena's hand and, closing his eyes, he bowed his head. Taking slow breaths, he prayed. He didn't try to force his mind to remember what he wanted. Using the techniques the therapist walked him through, he didn't grab for information or control it. He just turned it over to God.

Selena scooted closer. He could feel her against his side. He regulated his breathing, even as the images took form in his mind. Images of children. Children in dark places. He had to help get them out of the dark.

He raised his head. "I left the army to help you and your team. Everyone in your organization is special ops, but they're all retired from different branches. They're from different backgrounds, but we all have the same goal. Stop human trafficking." He opened his eyes. "You were my first contact."

Beto nodded, his face relaxed. He pulled a tablet out of his jacket and handed it to Xavier. "This has some basic information about past jobs, kids you saved. Nothing current. But it will give you an idea of some of the stuff we've done. What you've done. Maybe it will help trigger memories."

A slight tremor shook Xavier's hand. A simple swipe

and details of his work would be at his fingertips. He hesitated. Would this be the answer he had been looking for?

Would it take him away from his family?

Beto went on as if he wasn't changing everything about Xavier's life. "Do you think you're still interested in working with us once you heal? We'll have to have a medical release and probably a psych eval."

He reached across the small table and grasped Xavier's arm. "You've done a lot of good work. You're one of our best trackers. The way you can hack into any program has gotten us more information than we ever had before." He sat back and looked between Xavier and Selena. "What's said here stays here, right?"

"What do you know about the Colombia job?" His heart rate was hitting double time. This could be the information he'd been trying to figure out. Enough to get him started, anyway.

"I've got some names I can give you. Trent. Trent Morrison. He was your pickup man. But it wasn't a normal type of job. You were there to get a specific kid out. He was killed in the attack, correct?"

Xavier shook his head. "I have absolutely no memories of anything leading up to the attack or after. While I was in the camp, I was told my name was Pedro Sandoval. I had no memories, so I believed them. Was I working for him?"

"He was your contact." Beto leaned back. "He was super secretive. Didn't want us to contact anyone in his family. It was a nasty situation and he wanted to get the kid to the States. There was a family member here he trusted, but I don't know who. You had most of the information." He tapped his forehead. "It was all in your head."

Xavier had discovered the first week out that he had the skills to get in and out of any computer, but he had no clue how to navigate his own brain.

But something was wrong. What if the kid was still alive?

With a swipe of his thumb on the security pad, he unlocked the tablet. Chills ran down his spine. He was one click away from knowing more about himself.

Maybe this would help him understand why he left Selena. What was so important that he was running from his own life?

A handful of icons popped up on the screen. Selena had come closer; she had her head resting against his shoulder, looking at the screen with him.

She squeezed his hand. "Are you sure it's okay for me to see this?" She glanced up at him, then to Beto.

The man shrugged. "It's up to X. He's the one that wanted to keep it from you. We each decide how our families are involved. Some want the missions to be completely separate from their family. Others need their family to be part of the operations."

"Really?"

He nodded. "It's a hard job. Different people deal with it in different ways."

She turned to Xavier. "Do you know why you thought I needed to be kept in the dark?"

The confusion in her voice muddled his thoughts. Pulling her close, he pressed his lips to the top of her head. The scent of Summer Sunshine filled him. "No clue. I want to share everything with you, starting now. Between the two of us, maybe we can figure out who I am and what I was supposed to be doing."

She nodded and squeezed his hand.

He touched the icon that said South Asia. The file opened to several other files. Each was coded with a date and location that he understood. Excitement had his heart pounding.

He knew the code. He opened the file that would have been his first mission. Just the fact that he knew that gave him so much hope.

"Oh." Selena gasped. "Those are just little girls."

He flipped the device over, hiding their faces from his wife. His gaze darted to Beto.

He nodded. "It's safe. Those files are all the kids we saved. It'll have their recovery location and follow-ups." He shook his head. "There's still a lot of work to be done. But we're making a difference." Pointing to Xavier, he grinned. "He used to say one starfish at a time."

Selena took the device and turned it over. Her fingers glided over the screen, touching the face of each girl as she read her bio, before moving on to the next. There were a couple of older women, some teenagers and a few boys. "Each one of these faces has hope now that they didn't have before they met you."

She looked up at him, her amber eyes shining. "To think I was so mad at you each time you left." She looked back down at the faces again. "Do you remember them?" Her voice was low, barely audible.

"Seeing their faces brings some of it back. They were as scared of us as they were of their captors. It took a while to calm them down and to figure out that we were there to help them. But even then, some of them had no hope. Without the help of other agencies, they would've just ended up back there. Some of them were sold by their own families. There wasn't a safe place for them to go. Not without intervention."

She pressed her hand against her heart. "I wanted to keep our small town safe. That's why I do everything I do. So that my boys have a safe place to grow up and play and explore. But you...you were out there making the world a safer place for every child." She looked down at their joined hands. "Thank you for sharing this and for all that you've done."

His jaw locked. It was too much. He needed a break. Standing, he held his hand out to Beto. "Thank you for coming here and giving me all of this. Is there a way I can get in touch with Trent?"

"Sure." Beto stood and shook Xavier's hand. "I'll leave you all the info. Trent is undercover right now, but as soon as he's out I'll have him get in touch with you."

They watched him leave, then went into the house.

"It's time to call your dad," Xavier told her. "We need to get the boys back and get that tree set up."

"Are you sure? We can wait. Today's been... A lot has happened today. You need rest."

His instinct was to get mad and defensive. He was a grown man. He could handle a busy day and— He took a deep breath. There were a lot of new memories to sort through.

He took her hand. "What we need is to bring the boys home and finish what we started today. The tree goes up. We decorate it. What I need more than anything else right now is a little bit of Christmas joy with my family."

Two steps and she was in front of him. Her hands cupped his face. "New Christmas triggers coming up."

"Someone told me that was not how that word is used."

"That someone must be very smart. But don't bury all this new information away. You need to process it." She squeezed his arm.

The yearning to pull her close and clear his mind of everything but her was so strong. His mind and heart clashed in a battle for his life and he didn't know which way to go. Peace, he just wanted a bit of peace. But there was a job to finish in Colombia. He couldn't let that go.

She stepped away from him. "I also need to process this part of your life I never knew about."

He nodded. "Cali for the boys." The front door opened. He twisted her behind him.

"*Hola!* Anyone here?"

She smiled. "Buelita, I'm in here." She looked over at Xavier. "I'll have her help me decorate. Take some time to yourself." She disappeared through the kitchen door.

He stood there, alone. Images of people and places swirled in his mind. Needing to balance himself, he braced against the back of a chair. It was too much for now.

His family needed him without all the baggage. He could decide what he'd do with the new information later. Tonight, he'd celebrate Christmas with his family.

Chapter Twelve

Xavier tossed and turned, then punched his pillow for the hundredth time. There was no way he was getting any sleep tonight. Another week had gone by and no word from Trent. The sleep he'd been enjoying was gone.

Too many questions picked at his brain. He sat up and braced his arms on his thighs. The more he remembered the past, the more confused his life became.

He had to have left something here in the house. Selena had brought a few boxes to him, but none of them contained papers or notes. There had to be more written down somewhere that could fill in holes while he waited for Trent to resurface.

Standing up, he added a shirt to his pajama bottoms and slipped on his boots. The attic was a smorgasbord of forgotten junk. Flashlight in hand, he went up the stairs and pulled down the trapdoor ladder.

Moving with care not to wake the house, it took about an hour until, in the front part of the attic over Selena's room. He found it. A couple of boxes full of folders, notebooks and seemingly pointless odds and ends.

A knife that Damian had made for him. A collar that

Luna had outgrown. Some random rocks. If he'd saved them, there had to be some sentimental connection.

Sitting cross-legged, he closed his eyes and held the rocks. Rolling them from hand to hand, he let the weight and texture talk to him. Memories hit him like waves, threatening to take him under, but he relaxed. Giving in to the panic was a surefire way to drown.

After the waves eased, laughter filled the void. Selena's. She was a part of his memory, and he gave himself over to it.

The wind had taken her hat. Wanting to play the hero, he had jumped off his horse and slid down the sandy dunes they'd been riding along to the rocky beach below. The hat had gone out to sea, so he'd climbed back up to where she waited.

To escape his father, they had snuck out to the pasture and taken two of the horses for a ride. No saddles or bridles, just halters and lead ropes.

The wind had blown her long hair back and she sat on the back of a big gray. The sun had kissed her already golden skin.

She'd looked like a queen, even in her white tank top and cutoff jeans. Her bare feet had dangled as she'd laughed at his gallant attempt at knightly duties.

He hadn't gotten her hat, but he had returned to her with something. A rock. On impulse, he'd gone down on one knee and held the rock up to her.

"It's not a diamond, but it's a rock we can build our future on. One day this ranch will be mine. If you marry me, this rock and all the others will be yours. Will you be my wife?"

She had slid off her horse and dropped to her knees

in front of him. "I thought you wanted to leave Port Del Mar."

"I can join the army and make my own money, then we can come back here. My father won't be able to tell me what to do then. We'll see the world, then settle here, just like you want. And have all those kids you've already named. We can have it all. I promise. Say yes."

"Really? We're still in high school, Xavier."

He'd stood, pulling her to her feet and into his arms. "Just for a few more months. We'll graduate soon, and no one can tell us what to do. I love you, Selena, and I don't want anyone else in my life, so as soon as school's out, we should make it official. Will you marry me?"

She had grabbed his face and kissed him.

With the touch of her lips, the memory dissolved and he was once again in the attic. He opened his eyes and looked at the rock. As an seventeen-year-old, he couldn't imagine anything going wrong once he was out from under his father's roof. As a man now, he knew he had promised Selena so much more than he would ever be able to deliver.

She had been too young and inexperienced to know better than to marry a De La Rosa.

He tossed the rock back into the box. It landed on some official-looking documents. They looked important. Blood rushed into his ears. This could be it. Lifting them from the stack, he slid them out of the legal envelope.

At first, he couldn't figure out what he was reading. It couldn't be right. Numb, he scanned for a date. Icy coldness started at his head, then crept down.

Divorce papers.

Selena was going to serve him with divorce papers.

They were dated the week after he'd left. She had needed him, and he had gone to Colombia to save another family.

He wasn't sure how long he had sat there staring at the papers. But when he went to stand, his legs had gone numb. Shaking them out, he managed to get on his feet. She hadn't said a word about the divorce papers. Tilting his head back, he stretched his spine and filled his lungs to capacity.

He held the breath for a count of twenty before letting it out slowly. He wanted to barge into her room and ask her what was going on.

Checking the time, he rerouted his thoughts. He'd spend another hour going through boxes, then go to the kitchen and make coffee. She was always the first to wake up, and he'd be waiting.

Selena checked on the boys. Oliver was the only one awake and he liked staying in his bed, so she quickly changed him and put him back in the crib. He snuggled with his floppy pup and smiled at her.

Stifling a yawn, she went down the steps. The schedule for the day was already playing in her head. This was it. The big day she'd been planning and working on for almost two years now. Christmas by the Sea. It was her chance to prove to the chamber of commerce that Port Del Mar could be a year-round family destination and not have to put up with drunk college kids during Spring Break to make a profit.

Humming a Christmas song, she went into the kitchen. Turning to the pantry, she bumped into a male form. With a scream, she jumped.

He grunted, and her lungs expanded in relief. "Xavier

De La Rosa." She slapped his arm. "What are you doing hiding in the kitchen this time of the morning?"

"First, I'm not hiding. I'm fixing coffee for us." He spooned sugar into a cup and stirred it. "Second, this is the time of day when I know you'll be here. We need to talk."

"Did you remember more?"

"I was trying to put some loose pieces together. I thought maybe I'd left some stuff behind, so I went to the attic and went through the boxes stored up there."

Her mouth dropped open. "That never occurred to me. Great idea." She slid onto a stool and took the coffee he handed her. "Did it work? What did you find?"

"Enough to trigger more memories. More of my family. This." He placed the rock on the island.

At first, she looked confused. "A rock?"

He saw the moment the connection clicked. Her hand went to her heart and her gaze met his. "Your proposal."

"Yes. The rock I gave you when I asked you to marry me."

"Oh, Xavier. I didn't even know you'd kept it." Her fingers brushed the stone. "I always thought it was a good symbol for your life. Strong and solid, but able to roll and move from one place to another." She pulled her hand away. "You were my rolling stone."

"I made you promises I didn't keep. Told you things that ended up being lies."

Cupping her hands around the mug, she inhaled the richness of the dark brew. "We were babies. We had no way of knowing that so many of the things we planned were out of our control."

He slid the envelope toward her. "I also found this."

She put the coffee down and stared at the papers, then

back to him. She lost some of her coloring, but she didn't look at him. Instead, she glared at the papers. "How did those end up in your stuff?" she asked him. Or maybe she asked herself. "Oh. My dad. After we got word that you'd been killed, he helped me clean out your things. We donated most. But there were some things he said he didn't know what to do with, so he boxed them and..." Her hands shook. "I'm sorry."

"These were drawn up right after I left."

She nodded but didn't say anything.

"Did I know? Had we discussed getting a..." He looked at her, his eyes the darkest green she'd ever seen. All the light was gone.

"Divorce?" she supplied.

He smacked the counter, then turned his back to her. "I can't even say the word. Do you still want one?" He faced her, bracing his arms on the counter. "Did I want one?"

For a moment, she studied the steam swirling from the dark liquid in her cup. "We argued. You took a mission and told me about it the week after we thought the fertility treatment had failed. We thought it was over. I didn't handle it well. You tried but you didn't know what to say or do."

She took a slow sip of coffee. "Looking back, I know we needed counseling. We were so used to hiding our hurt and pain that we didn't know how to talk to each other. I thought you didn't love me anymore, but I wasn't going to ask. I wasn't going to beg you to stay. You had to make that decision."

"You didn't want me to leave, but you didn't ask me to stay?"

She rubbed her forehead. "When you put it like that...

I was so messed up, but I thought that, if you loved me, you'd know without me having to say it."

"What about now? Do you want me to stay?"

She gestured to the living room. "After seeing all those faces you saved? How can I tell you not to go?" Tears ran down her face. "I don't know what to say. How can I make that kind of decision when you don't even remember us?"

He came around to her side of the counter and pulled both of her hands against his chest. "I remember the love that I felt on the day I asked you to be my wife. You were amazing. I knew I didn't deserve you. All I had to offer was darkness and a stupid rock tied to the De La Rosas. Why did you say yes?"

How did she explain that to him if he didn't remember their relationship? She shook her head. "There's so much to do today. We'll talk about this later." Coffee in hand, she headed to her office. "You have the boys covered? I'm going in early."

"Buelita, Belle and I will have the boys on the float at the assigned hour." His fingers tapped on the papers he had showed her. "I shouldn't have brought this up today."

He pushed them away. "Sorry. Put this out of your mind. Don't give us another thought. Take care of your town and make Christmas happen for your boys."

She nodded but wanted to pull him close. Did he know he was one of her "boys"? From the first time she'd met him, she'd wanted to give him a life full of all the goodness he hadn't been given, but she couldn't lose herself in the process. Not like last time.

The corner of his mouth lifted. She wanted to cry for them both. So much had been lost.

"Selena, go. I'm good. You've always worried more

about others than yourself." He took a long sip of his coffee.

"But we need to—"

"Stop." He shook his head and gave her the smile that made the world around them vanish. "It's a big day for Port Del Mar. Go do your thing. We'll be at the Painted Dolphin at six thirty."

"Okay. Call if you need anything."

He lifted an eyebrow and just stared at her.

"Fine. Fine. I'm going to spread Christmas cheer." With a sigh, she went to her office. Xavier was going to bring their sons to the parade. It was a true Christmas blessing. She wanted to savor the joy.

But another part of her was worried about looking into the future. Would he be here next Christmas?

Chapter Thirteen

Xavier had never seen so many people in Port Del Mar. Half of them looked as if they had stepped out of a Dickens novel. In full costume, carolers sang, and the smells of hot chocolate and kettle popcorn filled the air. Selena had created this winter wonderland along the beaches of Port Del Mar.

He had told her not to worry about him or the discovery he had made in the attic, but it wouldn't leave him alone. Divorce papers.

The only reason they hadn't been filed was because he had died. He had known something was wrong, but what did he do about this? His therapist had warned him his memory loss might be due more to emotional issues than physical ones.

He sighed. There were moments he thought everyone would be better off if he had stayed in Colombia.

Belle bumped into him as she avoided a street vendor. She had Lucy in her arms. "That wife of yours is amazing. Look at this. It's taken her almost two years, but she's done it. Look!"

His eyes followed to where she was pointing. An acting troupe was bringing *A Christmas Carol* to life, complete with the Ghost of Christmas Past and Scrooge.

Buelita laughed. She was using the boys' empty stroller to walk the boardwalk, even though she claimed she didn't need help. "That's my friend Yolanda's grandson. His theater class is doing all the acting. They even translated some into Spanish. They've been practicing at her house. A live *telenovela*."

Cassie, Belle's ten-year-old daughter, held Oliver. The kids were all dressed for the grand float that would end the parade and take Santa to the plaza.

Buelita was dressed as Mrs. Claus and Belle was an elf.

As soon as he got the boys delivered to Selena, he'd go upstairs at the Painted Dolphin and watch the festivities from a safe distance. He'd be close by for Selena and the boys if they needed him. Not that she would ever admit to needing him.

The one word he kept pushing back today was hitting him hard. *Divorce.* But he didn't know enough to understand his reaction.

Today was about her and the boys, about the dream Selena had of creating a perfect Christmas, not just for herself or even for her family, but for the whole town and anyone who wanted to join in the fun.

He scanned the crowd. Colors and movement blurred. Closing his eyes for a moment, he calmed his mind. Slowly he reopened them, and the world came into focus again. Selena was responsible for all these smiles. Their boys were growing up in a world of childhood dreams. They knew they belonged and were loved. All kids everywhere deserved that.

Could he give up on the work he was doing around the globe and stay home? He rubbed his head.

"There you are." Bells jingled as Selena ran over to them. There was a frantic look in her eyes he'd never seen before.

He scanned the area for danger. He'd let his guard down. Where would be the safest place to move everyone? They were in the open and the babies and Buelita couldn't move fast.

"Xavier, I need your help. Mr. Gavord is sick." She looked over her shoulder, then leaned into him so close that no one could hear her. "I know you hate this stuff, but I need a Santa Claus right now. Mr. Gavord gave it a good attempt, but he's too sick to ride on the carriage. Elijah is too far away and everyone else has jobs assigned. The Mayor is in place at the front waiting for the parade to start. There is no time to find someone else. Please. I'll owe you big-time."

Leaning back to look in his eyes, she gave a tight smile, more like she was in pain.

"I don't have a suit." He had no idea what else to say.

"Mr. Gavord is here. He brought the suit, but he couldn't even get in it. The poor man."

Belle moved in close to them. "What's going on?" she asked in a whisper.

"I don't have a Santa." Selena looked at Xavier, her eyes big. "Please."

"Okay. But I have no idea what—"

"Just sit there and wave. You don't even have to say 'Ho. Ho. Ho.'" She stepped back and looked at Belle. "Will you get the kids settled?"

"Go. Go. Go." Belle shooed them away. "I've got the elf patrol covered. Are the horses here and ready?"

"Yes. They're stationed on spot seventy. It's behind the chamber's big gingerbread house." She grabbed Xavier's hand. "Come on." She dragged him through the parking lot and into the building next to the Painted Dolphin. Going through the back door, she didn't stop until he stood in front of a red-and-white suit.

"Thank you so, so much." Her words came in a rush. "I promise Elijah will rescue you at the end of the parade. He said he'd play Santa at the plaza. I knew that would be too much for you."

He frowned and was about to argue. He could sit at the plaza if that's what she needed him to do, but she was right. It wasn't about him not liking Christmas. That he could deal with.

She knew he was too weak to do the job for her. He hated that he wasn't strong enough.

"I'm good. So, the suit goes on, I sit on the float and wave?"

Nodding, she smiled. "It's not really a float. Belle will be driving a team of horses. We're wrapping up the parade with Santa arriving in a horse-drawn carriage. Buelita, the kids and I will be with you. If your sight goes or it gets too much, just let me or Belle know. You won't be alone."

With a grimace, he lifted the suit. "I'm not that fragile," he gritted out.

"Okay, buttercup."

Selena had no idea the muscles in her face could hurt so much. She had a whole new appreciation for beauty queens and royalty. Sitting across from Santa, she waved with one hand while holding Oliver with her other. He'd fallen asleep about an hour into the parade. Xavier had

Sawyer and Lucy on his lap. Buelita sat on his side, and on the other, Finn was hanging over the back of the seat, waving like crazy. Luna lay at his feet, watching the crowd.

Cassie was on the other side of her and Rosie sat in the front next to Belle.

The giant open carriage and horses were straight out of a fairy tale. The white lights that covered it made her heart melt. Until about halfway down the main strip, when the lights went out.

She almost broke down. The tears had been so close. It was a night parade. Santa's sleigh had to have lights. It could not go down Shoreline in the dark. But before she could freak out, Santa did something to the small battery and restored the sparkle.

As they turned the corner to the plaza, the snow machine kicked in and white flurries swirled around them. It was as if they were in her snow globe.

"Oliver. Wake up, baby."

He lifted his head and blinked. "Snow!"

Xavier let out a robust "Ho, ho, ho," and the kids all cheered. Buelita's eyes twinkled just like theirs. God's love surrounded them. Selena wanted to stay in this moment forever.

This was the stuff of her childhood dreams. Before they were married, this was the Christmas she imagined she and Xavier would have with their children.

She'd given up on those dreams a long time ago. First, it appeared that they wouldn't have children, and then... well, then her husband had been killed. The impossible was actually happening.

She looked at Santa and he winked at her. Xavier was

playing Santa and flirting with her. That was the defini-
tion of impossible.

The horses stopped at the plaza. A couple of the guys
who worked for Saltwater Cowboys were there, ready
to make sure the horses were safe. Belle jumped down.

Across the street at the library's back door, Elijah
waved at her. Carolers led by her father filled the plaza
with song, "Angels and Shepherds" ringing through the
air. With the help of Cassie and Buelita, Belle ushered
the kids to the space behind the plaza, Luna following
with the boys.

There was already a long line of kids waiting to see
Santa and get their pictures taken. Waving to them, Ser-
ena stood next to Santa on the plaza steps. "Santa is going
to refuel with some of Mrs. Garza's cookies before set-
tling in to take pictures with you all. But first he wants
to light up Port Del Mar with Christmas lights."

"Ho, ho, ho," Xavier exclaimed as he waved. And at
the perfect time, the hundreds of lights wrapped around
the trees came on in a wonderful flurry.

Tears burned her eyes. They'd always made a great
team. This was how she'd pictured their future when
they'd taken their vows. Before it had been derailed by
his need to save the world. A world that needed saving.

They walked across the courtyard to the library.

Was she being selfish? Had the divorce been due to
her hurt pride and feelings or had they truly grown apart?

Elijah opened the door, and once inside the confer-
ence room, the two men hugged.

Xavier yanked off the hat and beard. "I don't think
I've ever been so happy to see you, Elijah."

The men disappeared into a smaller room. After a few
minutes, Xavier and a new Santa stepped out.

"Thank you so much, Elijah." Selena hugged him.

Jazz took a couple of pictures of her husband, and then she took his hand. "Come on, big guy. Your fans are waiting."

Xavier sat in one of the large leather chairs with a heavy sigh. "Well, that was something I never thought I'd do."

"You did great. You even sounded jolly." She giggled. "You, Mr. Scrooge, saved the town parade, just like a hero in a good Christmas story."

She took his hand, but he pulled away from her.

"If I'd been a real hero, I would have gone to the plaza and listened to all those kids' Christmas wishes."

"It's okay." She crouched in front of him, her palms flat on his knees. "You and Elijah make a great team. We all do better when we work together."

He flopped his head back. "Well, at least I didn't have to lie to anyone."

"What do you mean?"

"For some of those kids out there, their Christmas wishes won't come true, no matter how good they are or how much they believe. You know that as well as I do. How many Christmases did it take you to figure out it was all a scam?"

Tears sprang to her eyes. "Oh, Xavier. It's not a scam. Christmas is hope. I want every kid here today to get a gift. There's a large team of elves to make that happen."

"And what stops their parents from returning those gifts for cash, so they can get more—" He lowered his head into his hands. "I'm so sorry, Selena. You've worked so hard to make this right. I shouldn't be here."

"This is bringing up some major issues for you. I'm not naive. I know that, for some of these kids, this doesn't take away the hardships they've had to live through, but maybe it will help one or two find some joy and hope. Sometimes that's all we need to keep moving forward. Trusting that God has us all in His hands. That's what you taught me. Part of what drives me is how your father raised you. Hardships are one thing, but your father was cruel and abusive."

He stared at her for a long moment. "There's so much of my life I wish I could forget, but you were everything good." His gaze went past her. "Why are we in here when all your Christmas memories are happening out there?"

She stood and sighed. "You're right. We can talk later. Will you join me? At least for a little bit? I know the crowds and lights can be too much, so you can come back here when—"

He put his cowboy hat on and took her hand. "Show me your Christmas town. Let's give my brain a few new Christmas triggers." He winked.

As they walked across to the plaza, people greeted them, including Cassie who had Sawyer on the harness so he wouldn't get lost in the crowd.

Selena nodded to the old-fashioned sleigh they'd brought in where people could pose for pictures against a backdrop of trees covered with fake snow. "Will you help me get the boys over there so I can get pictures?" He nodded. She watched him go and went to retrieve Finn from her father. Her eyes burned. Everything was too perfect. One lesson she learned well. When life was too good to be true, it was all about to go south.

Xavier paused as the words to "Silver Bells" stirred memories. Riff was holding Finn as they sang. This was

the life Selena had always wanted, the life he had promised her.

Would he mess it all up if he tried to become part of
it? Behind him, she laughed. Finn in his arms, he turned
to find her. She was talking to a young couple he didn't
recognize. They had a baby bundled up in their arms. He
looked at his son, already a toddler, and thought of everything he had missed in the lives of his triplets.

He had to sit. Finn was babbling about something,
but he couldn't focus. Nodding, he held the boy closer.
All the feelings he had for Selena bombarded his brain.

Each was tied to images of their life together. She was
his heart, his reason for everything he did. He had known
that, but now he felt it. The love, the joy, the pain and the
heartache. Everything up to— He closed his eyes and
tried to grab the last year before he left. But the memory eluded him.

"Xavier?" Riff sat on the bench next to him. "Everything okay, man?"

"I'm not sure." He turned to his father-in-law. "I loved
her so much. I walked out on her. I left. Why?"

The older man shrugged. "That's who you are. Some
things we just can't change about ourselves."

"Do you really believe that?"

"Like I said earlier, I don't give advice anymore." He
sighed. "But I'll tell you the same thing I've told my
daughter. You have to be true to what God has put in
your heart. If you follow that, everything else will fall
into place."

Selena waved to them. Finn pushed against him, eager
to get to her. "Mama."

Xavier put the toddler on the ground and he took off

toward his mother. Selena had Oliver, and Jazmine stood with Cassie and Sawyer. Selena waved at him to join them.

The shine from all the lights sparkled in her eyes. This was his family. Did the last few months before he left matter if they focused on the here and now?

He turned to Riff. "Did you know she had divorce papers drawn up?"

Riff grunted. "She was hurting when you left that last time. You were both hurting." He slapped Xavier on the shoulder. "But that was then. Today is a new day, so let's live in the moment. I would think that would be one of the blessings of losing memories. All you have is today. No baggage. Let all that go and enjoy your family." He stood and walked over to the sleigh.

As he gazed at his boys, the faces of other children came into his mind. Children he didn't know. Children lost, children who needed him. Something was telling him he had to go to Colombia then come back here and work things out. At least be a father to his sons if he couldn't be a husband to his wife.

The sounds of his boys' excited voices drew him back. Still in their elf costumes, Oliver and Finn were settled on a green-and-red-plaid blanket on the seat of the antique sleigh. But Sawyer jumped down as soon as Selena stepped back to take the picture.

"Cookie! Cookie!" he screamed, as he tried to run past the adults. Luna barked as she and Xavier cut him off.

He picked up the screeching toddler. "A picture for your mama, then we'll go and…" He scanned the area for something to do other than feed his son more sugar.

A few feet away, there was a tent where kids could make an ornament for the tree. He shuddered at the thought of glitter, but duty called.

He grinned at Selena as he sat the third triplet next to his brothers. He motioned for Luna to sit on the floor next to the squirming boys. "Who wants to make ornaments?" They all clapped.

Talking to the boys, Selena took several pictures with her phone. "Luna looks so cute in the scarf Buelita made for her. We could market doggy scarfs."

Then Sawyer pulled Oliver's hat off, causing the smallest triplet to cry. Finn tried to escape over the back of the sleigh, but Xavier was there to catch him before he fell to the ground. Chuckling, Selena took a few more pictures of the chaos. "I think they're done."

Riff put Finn on his shoulders and gathered Luna's leash. "I'll go get Buelita, then we can head to the craft tent. Does that work?"

"Yes. Very much yes." He turned to Selena. "Do you need anything else from us?"

"No." She stood in front of him and searched his eyes. "Thank you. You made today perfect. You definitely went above and beyond fatherly duty."

His hand settled on her neck as his thumb stroked her face. "Thank you for trusting me to help you." Finn roared like a lion for no apparent reason and Luna barked. The moment was gone. "I left my phone in the room when I changed from the Santa suit. I'll just go and grab it, then I'll help your dad get the boys to the craft tent."

Stepping back, she nodded.

If he could just let everything go and live in the moment, life would be easier. But his life was never meant to be easy.

Selena deserved a full-time husband, and he couldn't guarantee he could be that right now. He had too much unfinished business.

With a tilt of her head, she studied him. "Are you okay?"

"Yeah." Then he turned and left. It was easier.

Chapter Fourteen

Selena brushed the dirt off Oliver's jeans, readying him to go make his ornament. But Xavier hadn't returned yet. He should have been back by now. She glanced over her shoulder to check on Sawyer, who had gone with the girls to look at the miniature horses as they waited. A man she didn't know was crouching in front of him. Heart racing, she scooped up Oliver and rushed over to them.

He was speaking Spanish. "I'm looking for your father." He was holding something out to Sawyer.

"Excuse me, do I know you?" She took her son's hand and moved him behind her. The man stood. He was a little shorter than her with light brown hair.

Over the man's shoulder, she saw her father and Belle racing toward her. When they made eye contact, they slowed down, but didn't stop moving.

The stranger held his hands up and continued speaking in Spanish. "I was just speaking to your fine little man. I'm looking for his father. Xavier De La Rosa. I'm a business associate."

"What business would that be?" She took a deep breath to slow the blood pounding in her veins. It wouldn't do to jump to the worst conclusions. On the other hand, trusting him would be stupid. Her gut told her to stay on guard.

"I'm Juan Carlos Ramirez. I need to speak with him. I'm not here to cause harm."

Everything in her screamed to not trust him. Her heart rate ramped up again, and her skin suddenly felt too tight for her body.

"He's not here."

"I have come a long distance. He has information that I need."

Her father picked up Sawyer. "Do you have a business card? If we see him, we'll pass on your contact information."

Belle stood on the other side of her. "Do I need to call anyone?" she asked Selena. "Elijah? The sheriff?"

The stranger put up his hands. "I'm not here to cause trouble. I just need to speak to Xavier De La Rosa."

A warm hand gently touched her back and when she recognized the touch, she felt her muscles let go of the tension. She looked up at her husband.

He turned to Riff. "Why don't you and Belle take the kids to make their ornaments? Buelita's over there with Finn."

With a nod, Riff and Belle moved the kids away to the craft booth at the far end of the plaza.

Leaning into him, everything in her world righted and she could breathe again. Xavier stood there, glaring at the man across from her.

The stranger's glance followed the boys as they left, and then returned to Xavier. "Those are some very cute boys you have there. You must be a proud father. Chil-

dren are blessings reminding us of the innocence of life."
He held his hand out. Xavier ignored it.

Clearing his throat, the man briefly looked down before continuing. "Your wife just informed me that you weren't here. I'm Juan Carlos Ramirez. I'm hearing rumors you might know what happened to my cousin's little boy. Diego Puentes."

"I just arrived. I don't know anything about Diego Puentes." He held up his phone. "I was just contacted by a friend of mine that might help with this situation."

"My family is concerned about what happened to the boy. You were the last one with him."

"Like I said, I have no knowledge of this boy. But I can call the sheriff for you and he can help you."

"No. No. The law is not needed."

Luna stood rigid next to Xavier. To an outsider, her husband looked relaxed, as though he didn't have a care in the world, but Selena knew better. Every muscle in his body was ready to attack. This was not a friendly situation. Should she alert the police, or would that make this worse?

"Is there somewhere more private we can speak?" The man scanned the area around them. He rubbed his hands on his dress pants.

"No. I'm sorry. There was an accident. I have severe memory loss. I can't help you. But if you give me your information, I will pass it on to my buddies that might be able to get what you need."

She relaxed her shoulders and unclenched her fists. She was torn between wanting to run with the boys and not wanting to leave Xavier here by himself.

This man obviously had something to do with Colombia, and Xavier didn't have the memories to take care of the situation properly.

The stranger handed Xavier a card. "Working with my family can be very profitable."

He took the card but didn't say anything.

Xavier shifted so that he could talk to her without the man hearing. "Trent's in town with Beto. He left a message for me. Go hang out with the boys while I make the call. I want to make sure Juan Carlos is occupied before we head home."

Moving her head closer to his, she lowered her voice. "Is this dangerous? Do I need to call the sheriff?"

He gave her hand a slight squeeze. "No. Trent and Beto will handle it. I hate that he was here in your town because of me."

"You're not doing anything, are you?"

"No. Just calling Trent. Go celebrate with the boys. Keep them close. I'll be there as soon as I speak with them, and I'll let you know what's going on. Okay?"

She nodded, then headed to the boys. That last part was new. In the past he'd never told her anything about his work.

A group of kids ran past her, laughing. All the Christmas wonder in the world couldn't stop the roll her stomach was taking. This couldn't be good.

Selena sat in the dark, alone in the quiet house hours later as she waited for Xavier. After they had arrived home, he'd left to meet with Trent.

He had assured her that everything was fine, but she needed to see him.

In some ways, it took her back to the days of covert missions and long-distance trips. Except that this time she knew what he was doing. No more secrets. She sipped her warm tea, but it wasn't bringing its usual tranquility.

A distraction would be good right about now. There were seven stockings on the fireplace mantel. She had added one for Xavier. Each of their names were hand painted across the top.

The image of the perfect Christmas.

Luna stood, her tail wagging. Then seconds later Selena heard the door click shut. She put down her cup and unfolded her legs.

Xavier stopped in the doorway. "It's late." He grunted. "Or really early. Whichever way you look at it, you had a long day. You should be asleep."

"I never did sleep much when you were out saving the world. This is nothing new for me."

He sat on the sofa next to her chair. "Was it better after you were told I was dead?"

Before answering, she gave that question a lot of thought. "In some ways, yes. But then I had different worries. If I could have done something differently. How I was going to raise the boys without you. The business. The ranch. How I'd keep this big old house that needed so much work. There was no shortage of stuff to worry about. I did get better at turning my worries over to God."

"I'm so sorry, Selena."

"That man...is he a threat?"

He fell back against the sofa and ran his hand through his hair. "I hate that my work has brought any kind of threat into your town."

She wanted to point out that it was his town, too, but if he didn't see it that way, should she bother? Her body and mind were so tired. Holding her gaze steady, she waited for more information.

With a sigh, he sat up and met her eyes. "He's part of the Colombian family I was hired to protect the boy from. Trent made it clear to him that staying in the States was not the best thing for his business. He also confirmed that the boy was killed in the ambush. Trent believes his family was hired the rebels to attack us."

She shifted to the sofa. "That's horrible." Sitting next to him, she took his hand. "I'm so sorry. I know you were having doubts about his death."

He grinned. "That's what Trent told Juan Carlos, but we've been known to lie for a good cause, and keeping that boy protected is a good enough reason for me." He moved farther into her space. "I was right. He was with me. We had a plan to get him out of the country to his aunt here in the States."

"Are you serious?"

"That's why Sandoval and I switched places and IDs. I was about to run with the boy. Trent was waiting for us." He leaned back and shook his head. "Trent gave me all the details, then showed me the picture of the kid. I'd seen him."

"You remembered?"

"No. The boy was in the camp. I didn't interact with him, but I saw him. I thought he belonged to one of the rebels. He's still there or he was at the time I left." Excitement colored his words. "Since I can confirm he's with them, we can go in and retrieve him and get him to his aunt. She's waiting for the boy here in the States."

Her body went numb. This was it. He was going back. Everything inside her wanted to scream no. "You and Trent made plans?"

There was a quick nod before he stood and walked to the fireplace. The fire was low, almost burned out. "Basic plans. There's still information we need to gather, but between what I know from being in the camp and the intel he has, we should have enough to act within the week."

Everything inside her froze. "A week?"

"This is time sensitive, and we need to act fast."

"But you've only been here three weeks. The doctors weren't even going to talk about any kind of medical release until at least six weeks."

"I see my primary Monday morning and I have PT in the afternoon. I feel great. My sight hasn't blurred on me. The doctors have all been impressed with my recovery. I can't just sit around and wait for my memories to come back while that boy needs me to take action."

Her tea had grown cold, but she clenched the cup, needing the warmth that wasn't there. "When are you leaving?"

"Not sure. The end of this week maybe."

Her head shot up to look into his gaze. "You'll be gone for Christmas?" She wanted to ask him why he'd even bothered to come back, but she knew that was petty and just the hurt lashing out.

"This has to be a fast mission. I should be home by Christmas Eve."

She'd heard that before. Her whole life. Promises her father had made, then her husband. Promises they had broken.

They stood in the same room, but they were miles apart. "Well, I guess it's done. I'm going to warm my tea then go to bed."

He nodded. Then a thump from above them had them both heading to the stairs. Xavier put his hand on her arm. "Go heat your tea. I'll get the escape artist. If I need backup, I'll let you know."

He turned and headed up the stairs. She almost followed him but took a deep breath and went to the kitchen. They hadn't even talked about the divorce papers.

After warming the tea, she went to the boys' room.

The door was open. The sight brought a fresh round of tears to her eyes. It hadn't been Sawyer like they'd assumed. Xavier was standing with his back to her and Oliver in his arms.

He had hard hiccups as though he'd been crying. His little fingers were curled in his daddy's short hair and he lay against Xavier's broad shoulder. They swayed back and forth as her husband's deep voice sang their son back to sleep.

"It's okay, little man. Go back to sleep." Xavier kissed him on the head. That's when he saw Selena. He smiled. "He let me hold him."

"I see that," she whispered back. In the spark of his eyes, she saw the man that had been her whole world… but then her world had fallen apart. She hadn't handled disappointment and heartache well.

He was making plans to leave her again. Not just her. Now that included their three sons.

Her heart was ready to trust him again, but no way would she allow that to happen. She must be smart and protect them.

Lowering her head so he wouldn't see her tears, she prayed. God had gotten her through some dark nights and He would get her through this.

Chapter Fifteen

The week with Xavier and the boys went by so fast. They made cookies, watched classic Christmas movies and went caroling with the church choir. At the Wednesday night service, the Christmas songs had brought her to tears. She'd stood with her family. Four generations and her husband, the De La Rosa clan in the pew behind them. She had lifted her face and closed her eyes. God's love had filled her as she praised him with music.

At the end of the service, tears were running down her cheeks. Dropping her head, she prayed, releasing the anger she had been denying. Anger at God, at her father and husband because they hadn't given her the life she had wanted the way she had wanted it.

But standing here surrounded by family and all the love they gave her made her feel unworthy. She had been given so much.

That had been two days ago. Now it was Friday morning and she stood in the kitchen afraid to go into the living room and see his bag. She'd always hated the days he left, but now it was worse.

He wasn't ready to travel. The doctor had released

him, but there was no way he could be fully recovered. He was putting his life in jeopardy again, without considering what it would mean to his family if something happened to him.

Anger bubbled up. She braced against the edge of the counter as she looked out the window above the sink. She couldn't stop the tears.

She was a fraud. Just two days ago, she had asked for forgiveness, but the self-pity was back. She was feeling sorry for herself and avoiding the real issues.

He would be leaving again. Turning on the cold water, she splashed her face, tried to wash off the evidence of her sleepless night.

"Selena?"

She jumped. "I didn't hear you come downstairs."

Xavier crossed the kitchen and turned her to face him. "Have you been crying?"

"I'm good. It's the music." With one hand she wiped her face, while with the other she gestured at the song playing. "'I'll Be Home for Christmas' gets me every time."

She smiled at him. His mind was set; there was a job he needed to finish. What was the point of bringing up old issues, issues he didn't even remember? She poured water into her teakettle.

"I'll be back Christmas Eve." He rested his hands on her shoulders.

His warmth was so close she was tempted to lean into him. Why was she so weak around him? She held herself upright and nodded.

"Selena, it's been a great week. I don't want to leave you upset. Do you want me to stay?"

She scoffed. "How can I ask you to stay when you're saving children from monsters?"

"What do you want from me?" His lips brushed her ear.

She closed her eyes and prayed for God to give her the right words, because she knew the words she wanted to use came from her anger and hurt. "I want you to be happy. I want you living the purpose God gave you." Opening her eyes, she faced him. His arms slipped around her. "Truth? I am worried about your health. Your memories aren't all back either. We…we lost you once and we just got you back."

His forehead fell against hers. "I haven't had a headache or vision issues for more than three weeks."

"If you had, would you have said anything?"

Lifting his head, his eyes looked more gray than green as he searched her face, then looked away. He didn't have to say anything.

"I knew it. You'll never admit to having a weakness if you can hide it." Turning, she walked to the dining room.

"Selena." He was on her heels. When she stopped and looked at him, he leaned into her space. His arms were on either side of her, his hands pressed against the wall, pinning her.

She was trapped between his arms, but she wanted to stay. He had been her safe place for most of their lives.

"What am I supposed to do?" Raw and rough, his voice tore at her already bruised heart. "I'm falling in love with you all over again. I want you to give me another chance, but I can't stay here when they call out. I hear their voices, locked in dark unseen places, and I have to take action. I… I don't know what to do."

Her eyes glistened with tears. She wanted to give him

a bright smile, but she was sure it was a pathetic shadow. "I don't have the answers. We need different things. I do know that our faith has to lead us to the plans God has." Her heart twisted. "That might not be with us as a couple."

He looked down. "No. I don't want to give up on something that I'm just getting back." He spun away from her, both of his hands on the top of his head. "But before I can do that, I have to finish this job. There's this gut instinct that I need to do something. I think on one level I knew that the boy was still alive and in danger. I want to do this one job and then I'll be back. I just need to finish it. We'll talk then."

"This is who you are. I'm not stopping you. But you have to be honest with yourself. There will be another job after this one, and then another. There's no end to the monsters. Your job will never be finished." She took his hand in hers. "What you do is so important. I'm not going to tell you not to do it."

"What you do here in town is important, too. I might save kids from the big ugly hiding in the shadows, but you give kids a safe place to grow up and feel safe." He lifted his hands and caressed her cheeks. "Because of you, I know the monsters can be beaten. I was raised by a monster, but you showed me that I didn't have to be the monster."

Her hands slid across his jaw and cupped his face. "You were never a monster. You always said I was your light. But you, Xavier De La Rosa, were the lighthouse keeper who guided me home and kept me safe."

She smiled. "You gave me everything I dreamed of. Everything. I will always love you. I'm not going to stop you from doing what you have to do." She laid a hand flat against his beating heart. "You know what you need to do. It's here, between you and God."

He bent down and captured her lips with his. He poured all his emotion into the kiss, into her, not holding any part of him back from her. She wanted to weep at the rightness of it, but his career was always between them and what they could be.

It had been so long. His hands trailed down her arms, then back up. Her hand went under his jacket to pull him closer. If she held him tight enough, would he stay here with her forever?

His strong fingers moved to her neck, and then he pulled away and pressed his forehead against hers. The urge to cry burned her eyes.

Why now? For the first time since his return this was all him and her.

He was going to give her this, then leave? Lids shut tight, she bit down hard to hold back the crying.

"I have to do this," he whispered.

Her hand covered his. "I know," she managed to choke out.

The rough pad of his thumb rubbed the soft skin under her eye. "Look at me, *preciosa*."

Her eyes flew open as a soft cry escaped from her parted lips. "You haven't called me that since…" She bit her bottom lip.

He searched her eyes. "I'm beginning to understand how precious you really are. You'll be waiting for me, right?"

The feelings were too deep for words.

"I hate the sadness I see in your eyes," he whispered. "I put it there, but I can't figure out how to get everything done that needs to be done. When I get back, we'll talk. No divorce papers, okay?"

She lowered her head, then lifted her chin and looked him in the eyes. "You have to follow your heart. I don't know what this means for us, you and me. That's not a threat. I honestly don't know."

"Selena. I—"

The kettle whistled. Ducking around him, she went to the kitchen and fixed hot cocoa, stirring it with a candy cane. She shrugged. "I'm used to everyone in my life having other priorities. I'm not going to make you pick between me and your missions."

"I know you think I'll keep going out, but this time will be different. When I come back, I'm staying. This is the last job."

She shook her head. "You've said that before. Lying to yourself—lying to me—will not change anything." Turning, she looked out the window.

He moved to stand right behind her but didn't touch her. It would be so easy to lean into his warmth. To ignore all their problems.

"I never wanted to hurt you." He gently swept her hair over her shoulder, then let it slip through his fingers.

"I know." Bringing the mug of cocoa to her lips, she took a long slow sip before turning back to him. "The one thing I know for sure is that God has me, and I'm made of strong stuff."

He leaned in to kiss her again, but this time she sidestepped him. "There's too much unresolved right now."

He opened his mouth but then closed it again when her father appeared at the doorway.

"Are you ready?" Riff asked, his gaze shifting between the two of them. "Has there been a change of plans?"

Xavier shook his head. "No." He glanced at his watch. "We need to leave."

She wasn't sure if it was pettiness or self-preservation, but she stayed in the kitchen, clutching the snowman mug. Her heart couldn't take watching him walk out their door with his duffel bag over his shoulder.

"Daddy. Daddy," Oliver cried from the top of the stairs.

She set the mug down and rushed to the front of the house.

Oliver tried to climb over the gate, but Xavier was already up the stairs. "Hold up, little man. You're going to get hurt." Xavier swept him up and held him to his chest.

"Go, Daddy. Go." Oliver tightened his chubby arms around his father's neck. He was barefoot, and his pajama bottoms were missing.

"Oliver, baby. What are you doing?"

"Not baby. Daddy's li'l man." His cheek was pressed against Xavier's chest.

Oliver, the triplet who wouldn't let Xavier hold him, now clung to his father. They came down the stairs. She laid her palm on his back, feeling the tiny heart beating fast. "You're right. You're a big boy. Come here. Your daddy has to go."

"No." He turned his face away from Selena. "Go wif Daddy and Wiff."

"Sorry, *mijo*." Xavier pulled the arms from his neck. "Go with your mama. I'll be back for Christmas."

She took Oliver from him, but he arched his back and screamed for his father. Xavier moved away from the door and back to them. He reached for the toddler.

Shaking her head, she shifted Oliver to her other side. "Just go. The longer you stay, the longer it will take for him to settle down. Go."

Xavier's face was set, but his eyes were full of doubt. Riff laid a hand on his arm. "We need to leave if you're going to make it to the airport on time."

"All right. Oliver, I'll be back." He looked at her. "I'll be back."

She nodded and soothed her son. Heading up the stairs, she pretended she didn't jump at the sound of the car engine.

God had a plan and her only job was to love her boys and make sure they were safe.

Riff was silent as he steered his Jeep along the shoreline. Xavier tried to calm his mind and think of the mission, but Oliver's cries wouldn't leave his thoughts.

This is the right thing to do.

Selena understood that the work he did was important. How was he supposed to sleep at night knowing there were kids out there waiting for someone to rescue them?

How could he sleep knowing he'd hurt her?

He'd come back as soon as he knew the Colombian boy was safe, and they'd work it out. This wouldn't be like the other times. Or was he lying to himself? Would he need to leave again?

His knuckles flexed. The last time they hadn't worked it out, she had filed for divorce.

As they drove through town, every storefront was covered in Christmas decorations. Selena's perfect holiday vision had become a reality.

He'd go, finish this job, and be back before Christmas Eve. He tapped his foot and moved forward in his seat. Even though it was winter, people were still on the beach. They weren't in the water, just walking along the sand, enjoying the mild Texas weather.

The snow machines had been set up and fake snow covered some of the trees decorating the sidewalk. Greenery threaded with red ribbons stretched across the street from pole to pole.

He leaned his head back. *God, I'm doing the right thing. Right?*

If he was doing the right thing, why did it feel so wrong?

He felt Riff turn to look at him before he spoke. "He'll be okay. Once we're over the bridge, call Selena. She'll tell you. A quick escape is the best thing, otherwise it just drags on. I learned that early on when Selena was a baby."

Xavier wasn't so sure. He had almost expected it from the other two boys, but coming from Oliver... Just two weeks ago, his youngest son wouldn't even look at him. Now it just about broke him to hear the sweet little voice beg to go with him.

How did he pick between betraying his son and letting another little boy die when he could stop it? It was an impossible choice.

At a red light, a family crossing the road waved at them.

A tapping on his window startled him. Elijah stood next to the door and tapped the glass again with his knuckles. Riff flipped the locks. His cousin slipped into the backseat, then closed the door.

Xavier raised an eyebrow, waiting for an explanation. "What are you doing out on the street this early?"

"Well, that's a good question, because it looks like you're heading out of town with a duffel bag."

Xavier was tired of explaining himself. He was tired of letting people down. "I'll be back. I've got to finish this job…got to get down to Colombia and find that boy. He's alive and he has family here in the States waiting for him. They can protect the kid, but we have to get him out."

"And you're the only one that can do it." Elijah leaned forward, his hand on the edge of the seat, as Riff drove ahead when the light changed.

He didn't get it. "I'm the one that was hired to protect him. I'm the one responsible for him. He's alive and in danger. I need to make sure he gets out and that he gets to the right people. That's what I was hired to do."

"There's no one that you can give the information to?" Elijah turned, his eyes narrowed. "As the oldest, you felt responsible for all of us. Somehow in your head you're now responsible for every kid in the world."

"Not every kid, but this one. You don't get it. You never even left this town."

"Really? You're still the big bad older brother and I don't deserve to—"

"Stop."

"Okay. Fine. So what about the guys you work with? Your special ops buddies? Isn't there a whole team of you?"

Xavier sighed. "Yes. They're busy. There's a lot of cases. I was there, I know the people in this camp. How they work."

"And none of them can get this done? You've got the information, you give it to the right people, you follow up, you're doing your job. Without abandoning your wife and boys."

"I'm not abandoning them." Through gritted teeth,

he pronounced each word. "I'll be back, hopefully by Christmas."

"You're serious?" Elijah stared at him. "You think if you leave now Selena's gonna be waiting for you? You've been given a second chance, and you're walking away."

Xavier could see the disgust on his face. Elijah had never looked at him that way before. This twisted him just as badly as Oliver's cries.

With a heavy sigh, Elijah leaned back. "Man, I always admired you. Wanted to be just like you. You pulled me through the darkest days of my life. Because of you, I was in a good place with God. When Jazmine came back, I was ready. I was ready to be the man she needed, ready to be the father that Rosie needed."

Riff cleared his throat. "It's none of my business, but everyone expects different things from life. Maybe you need to back off and let Xavier and Selena work this out. She's strong and independent."

Elijah scoffed. "You're the reason she thinks it's okay to be second-best in her husband's life."

The older man's knuckles went white around the steering wheel.

Xavier resisted the urge to rub at the pressure building in his head. If he took a few deep breaths, the headache would go away.

Shaking his head, Elijah turned his attention back to Xavier. "All I'm saying is that I couldn't have done that without you. Now I have a better understanding of our issues. Instead of alcohol, you hide. You run around saving the world when your family needs you." Elijah sat back and gazed out the window. His disappointment and frustration filled the Jeep.

Riff stopped to allow a man to jog by with his dog. Then a young woman with a stroller followed.

Less than a mile and they would turn onto the bridge that would take him over the bay and away from the coast. Away from his family. Xavier let out a heavy breath and leaned his head back. "Those kids need me out there. Whenever I close my eyes, I hear their cries. There are so many."

Elijah sighed. "I don't know what to tell you, man. You're saving the world. But there's more than one way to do that. You have a family and if you don't think they need you, then you're missing the whole point. I learned the hard way that we De La Rosa men need our families as much as they need us, if not more. Your father isolated us, made it dangerous to need anyone. Xavier, you need them more than you know."

"I've never denied that I needed her. I might need them too much. I get too comfortable and then I get angry and frustrated. I can't do the perfect nine-to-five husband bit."

"Selena doesn't expect you to be perfect. She's proven that she loves your stupid self the way you are. Sometimes the most courageous thing we can do is just stand there. Being there for your family doesn't mean being the perfect hero. We aren't gonna say or do the right thing a bunch of the time. You stay, and you love them and then you trust God. You have to win her love. Earn it, and when you do, life will be better than you ever imagined."

There was a red light at the last intersection before the bridge. "Don't cross that bridge. God's given you a gift with Selena and the boys."

"It's who I am. I can't change." The bigger truth was that she deserved better.

"Who told you that? Because it's absolute hogwash."

Xavier glanced at Riff. His father-in-law cleared his throat and shifted a guilty look to the beach side. "People are who they are. We don't change." He mumbled.

"I changed." Elijah made a disgruntled sound. "I was a falling-down drunk who threw temper tantrums. God made me a new man. Riff, what made you stay here after a lifetime of being on the road?"

"Not the same. My daughter needed me. Plus, I was getting too old for sleeping on a bus."

"So, you changed. Someone needed you and you found a new purpose." He looked Xavier straight in the eyes. "I'm not telling you that you have to change, just to think why you say you can't."

"What if I do love her? What, then?"

"You show her by being there for her and living a life together, supporting each other. You spend every day thanking God for her and all the wonderful things she brings into your miserable life."

He opened the back door but paused halfway out. "We have a history of avoiding, running and hiding to survive our childhood. I hid in drink and drove the people I love away. You run off and save the world. It's a much nobler choice than mine, but it has the same results. The people we claim to love can't trust us to be there for them."

The light turned green and the car behind them honked. Before Riff could hit the gas, Elijah stepped out of the car with a little salute. He didn't give them another glance as he hit the sidewalk and headed back toward town.

Xavier closed his eyes. There were so many things that Elijah was right about. He loved Selena. Without her his life was hollow.

He had been running or hiding.

His cousin, his best friend and, in all truth, his brother had lived through the same horrific childhood. They had stood side by side as they'd grown from boys to men.

There was nothing to hide from him.

Elijah had just called him a coward. The doubt hit hard, creating a new rhythm in his head.

A screech of tires pulled him out of his thoughts. He looked up and saw a red blur appear from the left. He instinctively reached for Riff to protect him but before he could, the Jeep was violently knocked off its path. The crash vibrated in his ears. In his head, though, it was more like an explosion that lifted them off the ground. Screams and shouts mingled with the sounds of the jungle.

The boy was under him, crying. No, no, no. He was so close to getting home. He had to get to Selena. Hold her. Be the husband she needed.

It wasn't supposed to end like this. He didn't have his wedding ring on. She wouldn't know how much he loved her.

The detail of every thought the day of the attack hit his brain hard.

He wanted out. He wanted to go home and stay. Sweat ran down his back from the fires surrounding them. The boy cried. Xavier was trapped. He twisted to check the driver, and everything went black.

"Xavier. Xavier."

Blinking, he turned toward the voice that pierced his vivid memory. Riff. His father-in-law looked at him and Xavier turned to gauge his surroundings. He was in Port Del Mar. And it wasn't an explosion. It was a crash. A car had run a red light and hit them. It sat in the middle of the road, its front collapsed inward.

The Jeep had spun to the side of the road and now sat facing the opposite direction. Cracks spiderwebbed across the windshield. The passenger door behind the driver was caved in, the back window gone.

"Are you okay, Riff?" he asked, turning to the driver.

His father-in-law nodded. His hands shook. "It just came out of nowhere."

Xavier's door opened. Elijah stood there, all the color gone out of his face. "I saw it happen, but I couldn't— Are you guys okay?"

They both nodded. Xavier got out of the car, then jogged to the red sedan. Inside a young man sat, stunned, his hands on the wheel as blood dripped from a cut on the bridge of his nose. "I'm sorry. I just looked down. I…"

"You okay?"

"Yeah." He looked up, his eyes wide. "I just…my mom's going to kill me."

Elijah ran up next to him. "I called it in."

They got the car off the road and waited for the police to arrive.

He had been coming home. That was his last job. "Elijah, do you have your truck close by?"

"Yeah, it's at the Painted Dolphin."

"I need to do something. I need you to drive me across the bridge."

"After all this, that's all you can think about? Selena is going to—"

"I'm not leaving. But I need to get a few things before I tell her." He turned to Riff. "Don't tell her that I'm staying. Just let her know everything's all right. It's going to be all right."

Elijah scowled at him. "Are you sure you're okay? No one is this happy after a car accident." He pointed to Xavier's head. "Did you get hurt? Do you need to see one of your doctors?"

Xavier grinned. "I'm better than okay. Will you take me, or do I need to call Belle?"

"I'll take you. Where are we going?"

He winked at Elijah, then pulled out his phone to call Trent. He went to roll his wedding ring with his thumb, but it wasn't there. He wanted it back and to never take it off again. Selena would come first. She was his heart.

His mission work would all be from home.

While he talked to Trent and Beto, the tow trucks and police arrived. He slipped the phone into his back pocket and answered the questions for the report.

As they climbed into Elijah's truck, doubt twisted his happy mood.

Everyone knew the truth. Selena was too good for him. Playing father for a few weeks was not a lifetime commitment and didn't prove anything. The boys were so well-adjusted and smart, they didn't need him. Maybe they were better off without him.

He had been taught to be the strongest in the room, to never open up or admit weakness. The man who had taught him that was gone. He'd been wrong about almost everything.

Xavier sighed. "So, um…" Why was this so hard? "Did you have doubts about what kind of father you'd be when you found out about your daughter?"

Elijah's laughter filled the car. "Yes. And if you don't believe me, ask Jazz. I actually sent her away, thinking it would be better for them. I was scared. My mother abandoned us, I never even knew my father, and I was raised by Frank. But, Xavier, we're not our parents. Frank was the closest I had to a father and he was a miserable, lonely man who took all his anger and insecurities out on us. God didn't mean for us to be like that. We're not."

Elijah gave him a solemn glance. "And we have each other. Belle set me straight. We'd never let you do anything to harm those boys or Selena. Not that you would, but we have backup. We have each other, just like we did growing up. Your boys will be better men because you'll show them how, by the way you love their mother. By the way you treat them."

Xavier's heart lightened. He was far from being the perfect husband, but he could show his boys that he was strong enough to stand with their mother. Strong enough to get on his knees and give it all to God.

Now if only Selena would agree to stand with him again.

Chapter Sixteen

Selena parked the car at her house and rested her head on the steering wheel. It had been a long day with the city council and chamber of commerce people. Doug Mason had complained for over an hour about the Christmas event and how it had ruined the grass, and then he and Phyllis had got in a fight over the budget for the upcoming fishing tournament marketing plan. Usually Selena found humor in small town politics, but not so much today.

Her dad's car wasn't in its place. Xavier was gone... again.

Being hurt and angry made her feel petty. Those stupid arguments over trampled grass and advertising dollars were so pointless when children needed a safe place to sleep.

What she needed right now was her boys. Jazmine had taken them today since her dad was driving Xavier to the airport. She called her. "Hey, lady. Are you at the house? I'm going to come pick the boys up."

"Oh, I don't have them. Um, Elijah took them to your place."

"His SUV isn't here."

"Go in and check. Maybe there's a note. Oh. My mom's calling. Gotta go." She hung up before Selena could say another word.

Puzzled, Selena looked at her phone. "That was weird." With a frown, she climbed out of her car and went to the house. The boys were safe with Elijah, but where were they?

At the door she paused. On the welcome mat was a piece of paper with red scribbles all over it.

Picking it up, she flipped it over. In bold print was one word: *HELLO.* It kind of looked like her father's writing.

Frowning, she went inside. In the middle of the hallway was another piece of toddler art. *COME.*

With the two papers in her hand, she moved down the hall, searching for another clue. Her heart was racing. The paper trail continued at the entryway to the kitchen.

The word *TO* was surrounded by a purple design. That had to be Finn. For the last month, purple had been the only color he would use.

In front of the pantry door, she found *THE.* Looking to the mudroom, she saw the final paper taped to the door. It read *BACKYARD.*

She took a deep breath and made sure to keep her expectations down. Maybe her father had something special planned with the boys to remind her how wonderful life was, even without Xavier.

Easing the door open, she stepped into the screened-in porch. The toys had been put up in the wicker containers and everything organized. A beautiful poinsettia stood on the table.

Under the flowerpot was a folded piece of paper.

"Please join us by the gate. Love, Finn, Sawyer and Oliver."

A tear fell onto the paper. Her father's handwriting. Her family wanted her to be happy. Either her dad or Elijah had had the boys do something for her. How could she waste time being sad when there were so many blessings in her life?

With a smile, she tucked the invitation into her pocket and made her way to the stone sidewalk.

Standing by the garden gate, the boys looked adorable in their little plaid shirts and red suspenders. When they saw her, they ran. "Twees. We pwaned Kismas twees!"

"You planted Christmas trees?" She glanced up at her father. "What's going on? Where's your car?" Then she looked again. "What happened to your face?"

He touched the Band-Aid across the bridge of his nose. "Oh, we had a little bit of an accident. But we're all fine. You're back a little earlier than we expected."

Confused, she shook her head. "Accident?" She went down to hug the boys. "The boys? Who's 'we'?"

"A car hit us as we were heading out of town. The Hicks kid ran a red light. Not sure if the car is going to be totaled, but like I said, no one was hurt. I got the worst of it. Xavier don't have a scratch."

"The twee, Mama." Finn touched her face.

"Okay, sweetheart." Tilting her face up, she looked at her father. "Elijah was with you? I don't understand what's going on."

"He's stalling for me." Xavier came up behind them.

She spun on her heels. "You're here." Her lungs froze. He hadn't left. "Are you okay? Did the accident cause you to miss the plane?"

Standing, she held Sawyer closer. Anything to keep

her from reaching out to Xavier. If she held him now, she might never let go.

"No. It brought back a lot of memories, though." He picked up Oliver. "But we can talk about that later. Right now, the boys and I have something to show you."

She followed him to the side yard. Between the house and sidewalk were three small cypress trees, freshly planted. Each one was wrapped in lights and had a big red bow.

Oliver slipped from his arms and ran to the tree on the far right. "My twee! Feeds bwuds."

Xavier laughed. "We have ornaments that are made from birdseed so that they'll visit the trees."

"Look, Mama. Look at my twee." Sawyer pulled at her hand.

She followed, her brain too muddled to comprehend what was going on. The boys smiled at her. "I love these trees." She went to her knees. "One for each of you."

They nodded. "We wove you." Finn hugged her.

New tears burned her eyes. "Oh, sweetheart. I love you, too."

Finn ran to Sawyer, laughing, then scooted around the tree, only falling once. His brother yelled, then gave chase once Finn was back on his feet.

Oliver hugged her around the neck and kissed her cheek. "Don't cwy."

"It's okay. They're Mama's happy tears," she reassured him. She patted his bottom. "Go get your brothers." He grinned, then took off to join whatever game they were playing.

Tilting her head, she gazed up at Xavier. "What's this all about?"

He held out his hand. She took it and stood. He didn't

drop her hand and she didn't pull it away. "Have you postponed the mission?"

"No. Trent's going in. I'm staying here."

"What?" She touched his face, searching for any injuries. "Were you hurt? Is it your head?"

With a grin, he leaned in closer. She started moving in, too, but stopped herself and pulled away. "Xavier. You're scaring me."

Over his shoulder, her father was laughing at the boys as they tumbled around, trying to jump over Luna. Her head was between her paws, but her tail hadn't stopped wagging.

Everyone was so happy. It was like she'd stepped into an alternate world from this morning. He dropped her hand and touched her face, brushing back the strands of hair that had fallen out of her clip. "Right before the bridge, we were T-boned. It jarred memories of the attack."

"Oh, no. Are you okay?"

"I relived the incident. I mean, I think I did. I still don't really know what happened, but I remembered my thoughts. What was going through my head. I had it all wrong."

She laid her hand over his. "Was it horrible?"

"That's not what brought me back. My brain hadn't been telling me to get back and finish the job in Colombia. My last thoughts before the explosion had been to get back to you. I had decided that would be my last job. I know I had said that before. This time I was coming home to you to stay. My place, my home, my heart is with you. I love you and I want to be the man you need."

A heavy pressure squeezed her chest. "What?" He

couldn't be saying what she thought she was hearing. "Xavier—"

"Hey," her father yelled. "The boys are hungry. How about we go in and get some lunch?" The toddlers cheered, and he lifted Sawyer over his shoulder. "I'll take them in and you two can finish up your talk."

Her father looked happier and more carefree than he had in years. Her gaze stayed on them until the door closed behind the foursome.

She was afraid to look at Xavier. Things had changed too fast. Her world was shifting faster than she could keep up. Could she trust this new reality?

"Selena, I love you." He grabbed her hand and led her to the trees. "That last negative pregnancy test before I left. I told you it was for the best. I didn't mean it. I was lost, afraid and stupid. I just wanted you to smile again and I didn't think I could give you the happiness you deserve. I'm still pretty sure you deserve better than me, but I want the chance to show you how much I love you."

He pointed to the trees. "There's a reason for these trees. I wanted to do something for our first Christmas together as a family. Something that would last through the years. Years I want to spend with you."

She swayed as her blood rushed through her heart. Could she trust what she was hearing? The trees. He had planted Christmas trees with the boys. "I can't believe you planted them today."

"Elijah helped." His strong hand cupped her neck, the rough skin on his thumb gently caressing the area next to her ear. "I failed you. All you ever wanted was a family, a place where children could grow up. A place you could make into a permanent home." He nodded to the trees. "I'll be here each year with our family to decorate these trees. The roots will go deep as our boys grow."

"Oh, Xavier." She was so afraid to grab him. There had been so many times in her sleep he had seemed real enough to touch. She'd reach out to hold him, feel his warmth, but he would vanish before she could touch him.

"I'm going to be here for every memory going forward. I didn't understand that until I was in Colombia. Missing you so much it hurt." He wrapped her in his arms. "You had to be hurting even more and I—"

"I closed you out. Pushed you away." This time, she held him close. She closed her eyes and listened to his heartbeat.

This man had the power to make her feel safe. He also had the power to hurt her. Could she trust him again?

"*Preciosa*, you were hurting, and I left you alone. I failed you. But I'm here now," he whispered. "I remember you. I remember our love and the heartache. The day you told me the fertility treatment had failed. You were crying so hard, I was scared. I just wanted you to be happy."

"You told me that it was for the best that there was no baby. I didn't understand why you would say that. I thought you wanted children as much as I did."

"I did. I was stupid and thought if I could make you think it wasn't the end of the world you'd smile again. I'd have done anything to make you smile." His arms tightened around her. "I'm so sorry. I thought those words would help remove the burden you had placed on yourself. I didn't know what to say. Please forgive me."

"This is all too much. Just this morning you were leaving. Now you have all your memories and you're here planting trees." Had the temperature dropped? Her hands were cold and tucking them into her jacket wasn't helping.

Stepping back, he nodded to the little Cypress trees. "I know they aren't real Christmas trees, but they are close. I planted the trees with the boys to represent our new future together as a family. I love you, Selena. I have from the first time I saw you on the beach."

Needing space, she turned from him and looked at the trees that her sons had helped plant. Xavier said he wanted to be here, but… It's what she dreamed of, but fear was her weakness.

Coming up behind her, he pulled her against his chest. His warmth surrounded her. The stubble along his jaw was rough as he kissed her temple.

"Xavier, I'm just—"

"Shh. Don't say anything. I know it's sudden and you might have your doubts. You have every right not to trust my words. But I promise, I'm not going anywhere. Christmas soon. I have some ideas about the future, but for now, let's enjoy the holiday and focus on the boys. I know they're just words but let me show you how much I love you. Please, give me a second chance with your heart."

She needed to trust God and live fearless.

She turned in his arms and pressed her cheek against the steady rhythm in his chest. "You've always had my heart. It was my faith that faltered. What about the children you help? How can you—"

"There are other ways to help. I was running from myself, my legacy. Trying to prove I was good enough. I didn't have anything to prove. I'm not my father. I'm your husband, and that's good enough for me. God will show us the rest."

His lips pressed against her temple, and then he lifted

her chin with his finger. "I love you." His lips gently caressed hers.

This was where she belonged. Where he belonged. "I love you, too." Then she deepened the kiss. He was hers again.

This Christmas she would have her family all around the tree. It was a gift she had been too afraid to even ask for.

Epilogue

Rain drummed against the metal roof of the ranch house as wind rattled the windows. Xavier pulled the curtain back to study the night sky, then checked the news again. The storm was hitting hard, but it was predicted to clear out within the next hour.

It had been a cold, wet Christmas Day. He glanced over his shoulder. His nieces had the boys absorbed in a game they had received for Christmas. Selena was laughing with Belle and Jazmine as they put away the dishes Elijah was washing.

With his intel, the team had been able to go in an extract the young boy. He touched the green envelope on the counter. He had read the letter from Brenda Davies to the point of having it memorized. She thanked him for helping get her nephew out of Colombia safely. He could still get the job done without going himself.

"Did you wrap the pipes? It looks like it might freeze," Riff hollered from the living room where he and Miguel were watching TV. "We can get that done before we leave."

"I got it covered," Belle said, then laughed. "Get it? Covered?"

Selena groaned. "So lame. Do bad jokes run in the family?"

The branches of the giant oak beat on the side of the house. All the kids stopped what they were doing and ran to the sliding glass door in the living room. Oliver went to his mother and held his hands up. "Hold you."

She picked him up, and then Selena and Belle joined the kids and looked out into the stormy darkness. "Maybe y'all should stay over," Belle suggested. "We can extend Christmas till tomorrow."

That got the kids excited.

"Or maybe we should leave now before it gets worse," Selena offered.

If the storm didn't move on soon, Xavier's plans would have to be put on hold. Maybe that was better. Tonight was too soon. It hadn't been that long since he'd decided to stay. But he knew what he wanted. There was no doubt in his mind that this was where he belonged.

Drying his hands on a dish towel, Elijah bumped him, shoulder to shoulder. "No second thoughts, right?" he said, his voice pitched low so no one else would hear him.

"We can't do it with the storm." Xavier looked down at the weather report on his phone.

"Sure, we can. I can handle a little rain." He tossed the towel and leaned his hip on the edge of the counter. "What about your plans for the ranch? Have you been able to talk to Trent and Beto?"

He nodded. "They're interested. Belle's set aside time to meet with them and show them the property. I think it would work, Elijah. This can be a safe place for some of the victims that have nowhere to go. We've got the cabins and—" He dropped the curtain and looked at Elijah. "Sorry. You already know all this."

"I think it's a great idea. Not sure how we're going to fund it, but if God has the plan, it'll happen. You've got our support. Belle and I talked about selling parts of the ranch. We're sitting on a fortune with the coastal frontage, but we don't want just anyone moving in."

Their conversation was cut short when Jazz held up a bag of marshmallows and some chocolate. "Hey, guys, our bonfire got rained out, but we can move to the screened-in porch for hot cocoa and Christmas cookies."

Selena grabbed the tub of leftover cookies. "Buelita's already out there listening to the rain." She turned to Xavier and Elijah. "Want to join us?"

"We'll be right there." Elijah fixed Xavier with a hard glare. "This is your time. I'm going to the barn, so there's no turning back." He stuffed his hands into the front pockets of his jacket and grinned like an idiot. Then he headed out the back door, through the porch and across the field to the barn that was visible from the back of the house.

Selena managed to get everyone settled in a circle as she passed out the drinks and cookies. Cassie wanted to read the boys their new picture books.

It hit him again, for the umpteenth time. This was family, home and love. All the good stuff Selena brought into his life.

He walked to the far side of the porch and looked up at the sky. The rain had stopped, and he saw a sliver of moon peek between the clouds.

A hint of doubt danced down his spine. What if she wasn't ready? He was still a stranger to her. If he moved too fast, he could lose everything. He dropped his head and rolled his neck. *God, I'm handing this over to You.*

A hesitant touch claimed his attention. "Xavier? Are you okay?" Selena asked. "I'm sorry. We should have done a quiet dinner at our house instead of at the ranch."

"No. This was great. We had Christmas Eve in town. This was perfect."

Her loose bun was coming undone and a few dark curls fell around her face. There was concern in those huge amber eyes. "But the memories from the past Christmases with your father—"

He leaned in and placed a fingertip over her lips. "The past doesn't have any power over me anymore. My present is wherever you are. And our future is sitting behind you, surrounded by family. All those little ones. The next generation will have roots that give them the freedom to fly. For them, the ranch is a safe place to grow and land when they need it."

Tears glistened in her eyes. "I'm so proud of you. I hope the plans for making this a sanctuary for those in need works. It would be an amazing legacy."

"You and the boys are my legacy."

"Mama, look!"

All the kids stood up and went to the railing, looking through the screen. Even the adults stood to look out into the night. Miguel was the only one who hung back, a smirk on his face.

Selena turned and gasped. "Who—"

Taking her hand, Xavier kept his gaze on her face. She was staring, mouth open, at the lettering formed by tiny white lights that he, Elijah and Miguel had done early that morning.

"What does it say?" Lucy asked.

"Did Santa do that? Who's it for?" Rosie had her fingers intertwined in excitement.

Xavier's heart pounded so hard against his chest, it was hard to breathe. He couldn't tell what Selena was thinking.

He dropped to one knee and reached for Selena's left hand. He took the ring out of his pocket and held it up to her. Tears were streaming down her face. His lungs seized. Was she happy or upset?

He blinked and looked at the barn. In white Christmas lights, he had asked "Will You Marry Me?" But something was missing. He frowned. The next word, in colored lights, should be blinking, but it just looked like a weird loop.

"What's that dangly thing at the end?" Buelita asked.

Miguel laughed. "i think that was supposed to be a *g.*"

A loud whack filled the night and then the lights came on. Colorful blinking lights that read "again."

Maybe he should have done this privately. Their whole family was staring at them now. "Selena, I know it's been hard the last few years. It's made us both stronger and I know without a doubt what I want. I want to start every morning with you. I want to be by your side as we watch our boys grow. I said we could take our time, but time is not going to change how I feel about you. I want to repeat my vows to you. I know that I'm not perfect, but we're perfect together."

"Oh, Xavier." She crossed her hands over her chest. "All I ever wanted was you, and a family together." She glanced through the screen at the illuminated proposal, then back at him. "Yes. I want to start the New Year with you as my husband."

He took her hand and fingered her old wedding band.

"What are you doing?" she asked.

"I had another band made to go with your old wedding ring. It's to symbolize the new life we'll have together, built on the hope we had when we said our vows the first time." He took it out of his pocket and held it up.

"Oh, it's gorgeous." A tear landed on his hand as he slipped the ring onto her finger.

"I know that technically we're still married, but will you stand with me and repeat our vows?"

"Yes. Yes. Yes. The sooner the better."

The audience they forgot laughed. Once Selena looked their way, the tidal wave of well wishes and backslaps was unleashed. Elijah stepped onto the porch and the kids jumped him.

Everyone had an opinion, which they put forth the rest of the evening. Xavier kept an arm around Selena's shoulder all night. He had his wife back and he wasn't letting her go.

"Do you think Pastor Douse will lead our renewal on New Year's? I want to start the year strong with my bride."

"I would love that." She gave him a quick kiss. "Thank you for making this the best Christmas, from start to finish," she whispered.

He grinned. "Good cheer to all." He waved a hand toward the family. He turned to her and put both arms around her. "I love you so much. Merry Christmas."

And it was a very merry Christmas, one of many to come.

* * * * *

If you enjoyed this story, look for
The Texan's Secret Daughter *from Jolene Navarro.*

Dear Reader,

Welcome back to the Diamondback Ranch. In *The Texan's Secret Daughter*, I had another secret. I couldn't wait to tell you that Selena's husband was alive. I couldn't wait to get Xavier on the page. I knew it would be a tough journey.

Winning back someone's love and trust is not easy and it shouldn't be, but with God, Selena and Xavier were able to reclaim the lives He had meant for them.

Then there were the triplets. I had so much fun doing research into the lives of two-year-old triplets. I hope you enjoyed them as much as I did.

On a serious note, I want to acknowledge the work that inspired Xavier's career choices.

The heartbreaking truth is the work Xavier does is very real and needed. It was inspired by a group called Operation Underground Railroad led by Tim Ballard. With the work groups like this do around the world, children are finding liberation.

Thank you for visiting my fictional coastal town of Port Del Mar (Port by the Sea). This is the second book in the Cowboys of Diamondback Ranch. If you missed the first, you can read Elijah and Jazmine's story in *The Texan's Secret Daughter*.

Many blessings,
Jolene Navarro